Sam wished he could tell Kristen what he was doing.

Lying to her about the mysterious text message had bothered him a hell of a lot more than keeping it a secret from the rest of the police. She'd put herself on the line for him and his daughter, more than once. She deserved his trust.

She deserved the truth.

But he couldn't tell anyone what he had planned. Not until he had his little girl safely back in his arms. The past few days had turned their lives upside down, but one thing hadn't changed: he would do anything in his power to protect his child, whether it was from a mystery assailant or a mercurial, enigmatic police detective with a troubled past.

If only the phantom touch of Kristen's mouth wasn't still lingering on his lips.

PAULA GRAVES

CHICKASAW COUNTY CAPTIVE

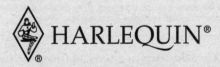

HARLEQUIN®

TORONTO • NEW YORK • LONDON
AMSTERDAM • PARIS • SYDNEY • HAMBURG
STOCKHOLM • ATHENS • TOKYO • MILAN • MADRID
PRAGUE • WARSAW • BUDAPEST • AUCKLAND

For Melissa, who surprises and challenges me daily.
I'm lucky to be your aunt.

Recycling programs
for this product may
not exist in your area.

ISBN-13: 978-0-373-74510-4

CHICKASAW COUNTY CAPTIVE

Copyright © 2010 by Paula Graves

ABOUT THE AUTHOR

Alabama native Paula Graves wrote her first book, a mystery starring herself and her neighborhood friends, at the age of six. A voracious reader, Paula loves books that pair tantalizing mystery with compelling romance. When she's not reading or writing, she works as a creative director for a Birmingham advertising agency and spends time with her family and friends. She is a member of Southern Magic Romance Writers, Heart of Dixie Romance Writers and Romance Writers of America.

Paula invites readers to visit her Web site, www.paulagraves.com.

Books by Paula Graves

HARLEQUIN INTRIGUE

926—FORBIDDEN TERRITORY
998—FORBIDDEN TEMPTATION
1046—FORBIDDEN TOUCH
1088—COWBOY ALIBI
1183—CASE FILE: CANYON CREEK, WYOMING*
1189—CHICKASAW COUNTY CAPTIVE*

*Cooper Justice

CAST OF CHARACTERS

Kristen Tandy—The small-town detective's tragic past comes back to haunt her when she's assigned to protect a child who has become a pawn in a deadly game of cat and mouse between the child's father and a faceless enemy.

Sam Cooper—The county prosecutor has more than one enemy. But which one is trying to use his four-year-old daughter against him? And can he trust Kristen, whose aversion to children is apparent, with his daughter's fragile heart?

Maddy Cooper—A mysterious assailant almost takes the four-year-old from her home, gravely injuring her babysitter in the process. Does Maddy's memory of the night in question hold the key to the kidnapper's identity?

Jason Foley—Kris's work partner worries that she's not cut out for working with children like Maddy. Will his doubts put Kris's bodyguard assignment at risk?

Carl Madison—The captain of detectives is also Kris's foster father. Has he let his love for his foster daughter cause him to give her a job she's not prepared for?

Nora Cabot—Sam's ex-wife hasn't seen their daughter in four years. Why is she suddenly so interested in visiting the child she abandoned as a baby?

Graham Stilson—The Maryland attorney is up for a seat in the U.S. Senate. Could the attempted kidnapping of his new wife's daughter be connected to his campaign?

Carlos Calderon—Years earlier, Sam successfully prosecuted the Sanselmo drug lord's eldest son, who was recently murdered in prison. Is Calderon out for revenge?

Darryl Morris—When Morris's son was killed in a collision, he urged Sam to throw the book at the man responsible. Has his anger at Sam for taking a plea deal instead driven him to desperate measures?

Chapter One

Blue and cherry lights strobed the night sky as Sam Cooper muscled his Jeep into a tight turn onto Mission Road. Ahead, a phalanx of police cars and rescue units spread haphazardly across the narrow road in front of his house.

He parked the Cherokee behind the nearest police cruiser, his pounding heart outracing the pulses of light. Ignoring the gaggle of curious onlookers, he took the porch steps two at a time and pushed past the uniformed cop standing in the doorway.

"Sir, you can't—"

Sam ignored him, scanning the narrow foyer until he caught sight of his older brother's terrified face. "J.D.?"

J. D. Cooper turned at the sound of his name. The look on his face made Sam's stomach turn queasy flips. "Is Cissy okay?" he asked J.D. "Where's Maddy?"

J.D.'s gaze flickered back to the paramedics working over the unconscious body of his teenage daughter lying on the woven rug in the middle of the foyer. "Cissy's alive but they can't get her to respond."

Sam's heart skipped a beat. "What the hell happened? What about Maddy?"

J.D. looked at him again. "We don't know."

The panic Sam had held in check broke free, suffocating him. He started toward the stairs up to the bedroom, where he'd last seen his daughter when he kissed her good-night before leaving for his business dinner.

J.D. caught his arm, jerking him to a stop. "She's not up there. We looked."

Sam tugged his arm away. "Maybe she's in another room—"

J.D. gestured at the obvious signs of a struggle. "Cissy didn't just fall down and hit her head, Sam! Someone did this to her! Someone took Maddy."

Sam shook his head, not willing to believe it.

A pair of detectives moved toward them, their badges hooked to their waistbands. All that broke through the haze of Sam's panic was the sympathy in the man's eyes and the complete lack of expression on the woman's face.

The female introduced herself. "Kristen Tandy, Gossamer Ridge Police Department. This is Detective Jason Foley. You're the home owner?"

"Sam Cooper." He bit back impatience. "My daughter's missing."

"Yes, sir, we know," Detective Foley said.

His sympathetic tone only ramped up Sam's agitation. "What else do you know?"

"We've searched the house and the property, and we have officers questioning neighbors, as well," Detective Tandy replied. Her flat, emotionless drawl lacked the practiced gentleness of her partner, but it better suited Sam's mood. He focused his eyes on her face, taking in the clear blue of her eyes and the fine, almost delicate bone structure.

Damn, she's young, he thought.

Foley took Sam's elbow. "Mr. Cooper, let's find somewhere to sit down—"

"Don't handle me," Sam snapped at Foley, jerking his arm away. "I'm a Jefferson County prosecutor. I know how this works. My four-year-old is missing. I want to know what you know about what happened here. Every detail—"

"We're not sure of every detail," Detective Foley began.

"Then tell me what you think you know."

"At 8:47 p.m. your brother J.D. called to check on your niece Cissy to see how she and your daughter were doing," Foley answered. Behind him, his partner wandered away from them, moving past the paramedics and out of view. Sam found his attention wandering with her, wondering if she knew something she didn't want him to know. Something bad.

Foley's voice dragged him away from his bleak thoughts. "When your niece didn't answer her cell phone, he tried your landline, with no luck. So he came by to check in person and found the front door ajar and your niece on the floor here in the foyer, unconscious."

Movement to their right drew the detective's attention for a moment. Sam followed his gaze and saw the paramedics putting his niece onto a stretcher. His chest tightened with worry. "How badly is she hurt?"

"She's been roughed up a little. There's a lump on the back of her head." Foley looked back at Sam. "There's some concern because she hasn't regained consciousness."

Pushing aside his own fear, Sam walked away from Foley and crossed to his niece's side, falling into step with J.D. "She's a fighter, J.D. You know that."

His brother's attempt at a smile broke Sam's heart. "She's a Cooper, right?"

"Mom and Dad have Mike?" Sam asked, referring to J. D.'s eleven-year-old son. Poor kid, growing up without a mother and now facing another possible loss…

"Yeah. I'd better call 'em." J.D. headed out behind the paramedics carrying his daughter out to the ambulance.

"Mr. Cooper?" Detective Foley stepped into the space J.D. just vacated. "We have some questions—"

Sam turned to look at him. Foley's gaze was tinged with pity disguised as sympathy.

"What?" Sam asked impatiently.

"What was Maddy wearing tonight?" Foley asked.

"She was in jeans and a 'Bama sweatshirt when I left her in her bedroom with Cissy," Sam answered, the memory of his daughter's earlier goodbye kiss haunting him. "She didn't want me to leave. Tuesday is extra-story night."

"We found those clothes in the hamper outside her room," Foley said. "Maybe she'd already dressed for bed?"

"Then she's in Winnie the Pooh pajamas. Blue ones. She won't wear anything else to bed. I had to buy three identical sets." He fought a tidal wave of despair. He knew the odds against finding Maddy alive grew exponentially the longer she was missing.

"We'll put out an Amber Alert," Foley said.

Sam walked away, needing space to breathe. The thought that he might never see his daughter alive again made his knees shake and his chest tighten.

"Mr. Cooper?" The sympathy in Foley's voice was almost more than Sam could bear.

"I need a minute," Sam said.

"Sure. Take all the time you need." Foley stepped away. A few feet away, Sam saw the female detective edge toward the staircase. Her eyes met his briefly, her expression grim. Then she turned and headed up the stairs.

Sam's heart squeezed into a knot. Take all the time he needed? Time was the one thing he didn't have. Not if he wanted to find his child alive.

THE HOUSE WAS CLEAN BUT lived-in, the carpet runner in the upstairs hallway slightly askew, as if someone had hit it at a run. Kristen Tandy moved past Mark Goddard, one of the two uniformed officers tasked with evidence collection, and crossed to a door standing slightly ajar. "Checked in here?" she asked.

Goddard looked up at her. "It's a storage area. Full of boxes. Didn't look like much had been touched, but I'll get to it before we leave."

She donned a pair of latex gloves. "Can I take a look?"

Goddard frowned. "Do you have to?"

But she'd already opened the door and flicked on the light.

Inside, the room was a mess. Stacks of boxes, mostly full, filled the spare bedroom. The Coopers hadn't been living here long, she guessed. Hadn't finished unpacking from the move.

"Maddy?" She stopped and listened. She heard no response, but the hairs on the back of her neck prickled. She stepped deeper into the room, squeezing between two stacks of boxes. "Are you in here?"

There was still no answer, but Kristen thought she heard a noise behind the boxes ahead. She froze in place, her head cocked. The sound of Goddard at work just outside the room mingled with a faint hum of conversation from downstairs.

"When I was a little girl, my favorite game was hide-and-seek." She formed the words from her frozen lips. "I was good at it, you see, because I was so little.

I could go places nobody else could go. So they never, ever found me until I was ready to be found."

She eased forward, past a large box in the middle of the room, ignoring the tremble in her belly. "I bet you're good at hiding, too, aren't you, Maddy?"

A faint rustling noise came from the back of the room. Beyond the stack of boxes in front of her, she spotted a door. The closet, she guessed.

"My name is Kristen Tandy. I'm a police officer. I came here to help your cousin Cissy."

A faint hiccough sent a ripple of triumph racing through Kristen's gut, followed quickly by a rush of sheer dread. Taking a bracing breath, she pushed aside a box to get to the closet and pulled open the door.

Four-year-old Maddy Cooper gazed up at Kristen with tear-stained green eyes, her face damp and flushed. "I want my Daddy," she whimpered.

Kristen crouched in front of Maddy, helping her to her feet. The little girl's hands were soft and tiny, and up close, she smelled sweet. Kristen felt her knees wobble and she put one hand on the door frame to steady herself.

Do your job, Tandy.

She looked Maddy over quickly. No obvious signs of injury, she noted with almost crushing relief. "Are you okay, Maddy? Do you hurt anywhere?"

"Kristen?" Foley called from somewhere behind them.

Maddy Cooper flung herself at Kristen, her arms

tightening around her. The little girl buried her tear-damp face in Kristen's neck, shaking with fear.

"It's okay," she soothed, fighting the primal urge to push the little girl away and run as fast and as far as she could—the way she felt every time she was this close to a child. Instead, she picked Maddy up and turned to face her partner. The scent of baby shampoo filled her lungs, making her feel weak, but she clung to her equilibrium.

Sam Cooper stood by Foley, staring at her with eyes full of shock and fragile hope. "Maddy?"

At the sound of her father's voice, Maddy wriggled to get away. Kristen put her down, and the child weaved through the stacks of boxes to reach her father.

He scooped her into his arms and smothered her face with kisses. "Oh, baby, are you okay?" Sam held his daughter away to get a good look.

Kristen looked away, a powerful ache spreading like poison in her chest.

"The bad man hurt Cissy!" Maddy wailed.

"I know, baby, but the bad man is gone now. And Cissy's getting help. It'll be all right now, okay?" Out of the corner of her eye, Kristen saw Sam Cooper thumb away the tears spilling from his daughter's eyes.

"Mr. Cooper, we need to ask Maddy—" Foley began.

"Enough, Foley," Kristen said flatly, joining them in the doorway. "You might want to take her to the hospital, too, let a doctor check her over," she said to Sam. "We'll talk to you soon." She grabbed her partner's arm, tugging him with her as she headed out of the room. She couldn't stay there one minute longer, she knew.

Foley stopped in the middle of the hallway. "How the hell did you know—?"

"Kids like to play hide-and-seek," she said, moving ahead of him down the hallway.

She knew from experience.

HOSPITALS HAD A SMELL TO THEM, a strange mix of antiseptic and disease that made Kristen's skin crawl. A doctor had once told her that knowing the reason behind an irrational aversion was the key to overcoming it. But knowing why she hated hospitals hadn't done much to cure Kristen of her phobia.

The doctors were still examining the two Cooper girls. Across from where she and Jason Foley stood, the girls' grandparents sat in aluminum-and-vinyl chairs backed up against the hallway outside the emergency treatment bays. The elder Coopers flanked a scared-looking boy of eleven or so— Cissy's brother, Michael.

"Why are we here?" Kristen asked Foley softly. "We should be back at the crime scene."

Foley slanted a gaze toward the grandparents before speaking in a whisper. "The girls saw their attacker."

"One of them has a cracked skull and the other

is practically a baby," Kristen shot back, apparently louder than she realized, for Mrs. Cooper sent a pained look her way. Kristen took a few steps away from the family, waiting for Foley to catch up with her before she added, "We should be supervising the evidence retrieval."

"Goddard's perfectly capable of that," Foley said. "The answers are here with the girls."

Kristen stopped arguing, mostly because she knew her desire to leave had less to do with good police work and more to do with her need to get the hell out of this hospital.

The doors to the Emergency wing opened, ushering in a cool night breeze and two men dressed in jeans and T-shirts. They were tall and dark-haired, clearly related to Sam Cooper and his brother J.D. The two men looked so alike, Kristen wondered if they were twins.

The one in the dark blue T-shirt caught sight of the elder Coopers. "Mom!" He hurried to her side and crouched by the chair. "I got your voice mail. Any word?"

Mrs. Cooper shook her head. "We're still waiting to hear. Sam and J.D. went back there with the kids. Cissy was still unconscious when she came in."

"What about Maddy?"

"She seems okay, but Sam wanted her looked over anyway."

The other man ruffled the dark hair of the young

boy sandwiched between the grandparents, hunkering down until he was eye level with the child. "How you holdin' up, sport?"

Michael managed a faint smile. "I'm okay, Uncle Gabe."

The man in the blue T-shirt caught Kristen watching. His gaze settled on the back of Kristen's right hand for a second. She saw recognition as he raised his blue eyes to meet hers.

Kristen ignored the look, but Foley flashed his badge at the newcomers, so she had no choice but to follow.

Foley introduced himself. "You're the girls' uncles?"

The man in the blue T-shirt shook the hand Foley offered. "Jake Cooper. Sam and J.D. are my brothers. This is my brother Gabe." He nodded toward the man who had to be his twin.

Foley introduced her. "This is Detective Kristen Tandy."

Jake's gaze slanted toward the scar on her hand. "I know."

She squelched the urge to stick her hand in her pocket. "Detective Foley and I are investigating the case."

"So I gathered." He looked from Kristen to Foley and back. "What the hell happened at Sam's house?"

"That's what we'd like to ask your nieces."

"Mom says Cissy's still unconscious and

Maddy's gotta be traumatized. Can't it wait till morning?"

"The sooner we know what happened, the sooner we find who did it and stop it from happening again," Foley said soothingly.

"Sam!" Mrs. Cooper's voice drew their attention. Kristen saw Sam Cooper coming down the hallway, his daughter perched on his hip. Maddy had red-rimmed eyes and a slightly snotty nose, but apparently she'd received a clean bill of health.

Sam locked gazes with Kristen. One dark brow ticked upward before he looked back at his mother.

As Mrs. Cooper reached for the little girl, Maddy clung to her father, tightening her grip around his neck. Sam gave his mother an apologetic look and kissed her forehead, then crossed to Kristen and Foley. "I thought you'd still be at the house."

"We were hoping to talk to the girls," Foley said.

"Cissy's still unconscious. They've called in a helicopter to take her to Birmingham." Sam's eyes darkened with anger. "If I ever get my hands on the son of a bitch who did this—"

"What about your daughter?" Foley pressed.

Sam looked at Kristen rather than Foley. "Can't it wait?"

She wanted to say yes. The last thing she wanted to do was spend any more time with Sam Cooper's little girl. But questions had to be asked, and for better or worse, she and Foley were the ones who'd been assigned to ask them. "I think the sooner we can talk to her, the more we'll get from her, while it's fresh in her mind."

He looked at her for a long moment, his expression hard to read. It softened a bit, finally, and he gave a short nod.

Foley glanced at Kristen, a question in his eyes.

"I'll talk to the family," she said. "You handle the kid."

Sam Cooper looked at Kristen through narrowed eyes, his irritation evident. "Don't like children?"

"They don't like me," Kristen answered shortly, wondering why his clear disapproval bothered her so much. "Foley has kids. He knows how to handle them."

Sam's expression darkened further, but his next words were directed at his daughter. "Maddy, this is Detective Foley. He wants to ask you some questions."

Maddy buried her face in her father's neck and shook her head. "No, Daddy!"

"Look, why don't we wait until tomorrow—" Sam began.

"The sooner we do this, the more she'll remember," Foley said. He took a step toward Maddy, softening his voice. "Maddy, sweetheart? I have a little girl just your age. Do you want to see a picture of her?"

"No!" Maddy's voice was muffled by her father's collar.

Foley looked at Kristen, his expression helpless. "You give it a try."

"No," Kristen said in unison with Sam.

Foley arched one eyebrow.

"She doesn't like kids." Sam's voice tightened.

"They don't like me," Kristen repeated, annoyed.

"Maddy, will you talk to Detective Tandy?" Foley asked, ignoring them both.

Maddy turned her head slightly, peeking out from under her father's chin at Kristen. "Her?"

Foley nodded.

Maddy pressed her face against her father's throat again, to Kristen's relief. But a moment later, the little girl nodded, and Kristen's heart sank. No way to avoid it now.

With resignation, she gestured toward the emergency room waiting area. "Let's find a quiet corner."

Sam Cooper gave her a warning look, as if he suspected the sole purpose of the requested interview was to further traumatize his daughter. She ignored his clear discomfort and led the way to the chairs tucked into the corner of the waiting room. Sam settled into one of the chairs, Maddy curled on his lap. Kristen pulled her chair around to face them. Maddy gazed back at her with solemn green eyes, her face still pink from crying. Teardrops glittered on her long lashes like diamonds.

"You saw the bad man who hurt Cissy, didn't you, Maddy?"

She heard Sam's soft inhalation but ignored it, keeping her eyes on the little girl. Slowly, Maddy nodded.

"Was he tall like your daddy?"

Maddy shook her head. She lifted one thumb to her mouth and laid it on her lower lip but didn't start sucking it. She craned her head to look up at her father.

The look of heartbroken love Sam Cooper gave his daughter made Kristen's breath catch. She looked away, a phantom pain jabbing her under her rib cage like a knife. Licking her lips, she pressed on. "So he wasn't tall. Was he short like me?" She stood up so Maddy could see her height.

The little girl considered the question for a moment, then shook her head again. "Bigger."

"Was he skinny like Uncle J. D.?" Sam asked.

"No, Daddy. Like Uncle Aaron."

Sam met Kristen's eyes over the top of his daughter's head. "My brother Aaron. You may know him—he's a Chickasaw County Sheriff's Deputy. A little taller than me, built like a bulldog. Played football at 'Bama till he blew out his knee."

"Yeah, I've met him before," Kristen said. She turned her attention back to Maddy. "So he's shorter than your daddy and about your Uncle Aaron's size. Did you see his hair color?"

She shook her head. "Had a daddy hat."

Kristen looked to Sam for translation.

He gave a helpless shrug. "I guess she means a baseball cap. That's the only kind of hat I ever wear."

Maddy looked up at her father again, her eyes

welling up with new tears. "He made Cissy cry, Daddy."

Sam's eyes glittered as he stroked his daughter's dark curls. "I know, baby. That's why we need to find out who he is and make sure he doesn't ever do that again." He looked at Kristen. "I don't think she remembers much about it."

"Did you notice anything special about him? Did he have freckles or moles or scars—?" With a bracing breath, Kristen held out her right hand and showed it to Maddy. "This is a scar, Maddy. See that?"

Maddy looked solemnly at the burned skin on the back of Kristen's hand, then up at Kristen. "Does it hurt?"

"Not anymore." She avoided Sam's gaze. "Did the man have anything like this?"

Maddy shook her head.

"What happened?" Sam's gaze lingered on the scar burned into her hand.

She looked up, surprised. He didn't know? She forced her gaze back to Maddy, ignoring Sam's question. "How did you get into the closet, Maddy?"

"Cissy told me to run so I runned." Her little brow furrowed. "I couldn't get the back door to open."

"Locked," Sam said. "She doesn't know how to unlock it."

"So I runned up to the secret place."

A chill darted up Kristen's spine, scattering goose bumps along her back and arms. Her stomach twisted, a sinking sensation filling her insides, but she pressed on. "The closet was the secret place?"

Maddy nodded. "Nobody ever finded me there."

"Cissy plays hide-and-seek with her sometimes. I guess she's so small she doesn't have any trouble squeezing in there behind the boxes." Sam's gaze moved away from hers, settling on something behind her. She turned to see J.D. Cooper coming into the waiting area, his face pale and drawn.

"Do you think you could watch Maddy a second?" Sam asked Kristen. He ruffled his daughter's hair. "Can you sit here with Detective Tandy for me, baby? I'm just going over there to talk to Uncle J.D., okay?"

Kristen wanted to argue, but the little girl had already climbed down from her father's lap and settled onto a seat beside Kristen, looking up at her with warm green eyes.

"Do you like to color?" she asked Kristen.

"Yeah, I do," Kristen answered, wishing she were anywhere else in the world.

"THEY'RE TRANSFERRING HER to Birmingham," J.D. was telling the others as Sam walked up. His voice sounded faint and weary. "They're afraid she's got some bleeding in her brain and they're not set up to handle that here. The helicopter should be here any minute."

"Is she gonna be okay, Dad?" Michael asked J.D., his eyes wide with fear.

J.D. hugged the boy. "She's going to be in the best hospital around. The doctors there are going to take good care of her, Mike. I promise." He looked at his mother. "Y'all keep Mike here, okay? I'll call with any word."

"I'm going with you," Gabe said.

"Thanks, man." J.D. turned at the sound of wheels rolling across the linoleum floor behind him. At the same time, Sam heard the first faint *whump-whump* of helicopter blades beating in the distance.

"Mr. Cooper, Life-Flight will be landing any moment." A nurse in a pair of blue scrubs stepped away from the gurney carrying Cissy and crossed to J. D.'s side. "There won't be room for you in the helicopter, so if you'd like to get a head start, we'll take good care of her until they get here."

J.D. looked at Sam. "I'll call when I know something."

Sam gave his brother a hug. "She's a fighter."

J.D. managed a weak smile and repeated the familiar old mantra. "She's a Cooper." He headed out the door, Gabe on his heels. Jake moved up next to Sam, watching them go.

"Hell of a night," Jake murmured. He looked over his shoulder at Maddy and the detective. "I see little Mad Dog has made a new friend."

Sam followed his brother's gaze to find Maddy leaning against Detective Tandy's arm. Tandy was sitting stiffly, gazing down at the child with a hint of alarm, but Maddy didn't seem to care. "Detective Tandy apparently isn't the maternal sort," he murmured.

"Can't blame her," Jake said. "She's got no reason to think much of motherhood."

Sam looked at his brother. "What do you mean?"

Jake looked taken aback. "Don't you know who she is?"

Sam shook his head. "Should I?"

"Oh, that's right—you'd already left town when that all went down." Jake lowered his voice. "Fifteen years ago, Molly Jane Tandy brutally killed four of her five children."

Sam looked across the waiting room at Kristen Tandy, his stomach tightening. The scar on the back of her hand made sudden, horrifying sense. "My God."

"Kristen Tandy was the oldest. She was thirteen. She's also the only one who survived."

Chapter Two

The space behind the cellar wall was almost too small to hold her, but she squeezed through the narrow opening and pulled the loose board over the gap, trying to slow her ragged breathing. Pain tore at her insides, stronger and bloodier than the cuts on her palms and fingers, more wretched than the searing ache on the back of her hand where the hot spatula had branded her. She had pressed her wounded hands to her body as she ran, terrified of leaving a blood trail for Mama to follow.

She held her breath, lungs aching, and listened. The angry shouts had died away a few minutes ago, the only sounds in the now-still house were the soft *thud-thud* of footfalls on the kitchen floor above.

Her mind was filled with images too grotesque, too profane to process. A whimper hammered against her throat but she crushed it ruthlessly, determined to remain soundless.

She heard Mama's hoarsened voice from the kitchen above. "Kristy, I know you're still here. Nobody goes outside today. Come here to Mama."

Kristen pressed her forehead to the cold brick wall behind the panel and prayed without words, a mindless, desperate plea for mercy and help.

The door to the cellar opened.

Kristen jerked awake, her heart pounding. She scraped her hair back from her sweaty brow and stared at the shadowy shapes in her darkened bedroom, half-afraid one of them would move. But everything remained quiet and still.

On her bedside table, green glowing numbers on her alarm clock read 5:35 a.m. She'd managed about four hours of sleep. More than she'd expected.

She switched on the bedside lamp, squinting against the sudden light. Her fingers itched to grab the cell phone lying on the table next to her, but she squelched the urge. Foley wouldn't appreciate a predawn call, and it wasn't as if she had anything to tell him anyway.

As of midnight, when Kristen and Foley called it a night, Cissy Cooper was still unconscious in a Birmingham hospital, her prognosis guarded and uncertain. Sam Cooper and his daughter were spending the next few nights at his parents' place on Gossamer Lake. The crime scene had offered up plenty for the lab to sift through but no obvious smoking gun. And Kristen had at least two more hours to wait before she could decently start following up on the few leads she and Foley had to work with.

She'd start with the ex-wife, she decided sleepily as she stepped into the shower and turned the spray on hot and strong. Sam Cooper had seemed certain the former Mrs. Cooper wasn't a suspect, but Kristen believed in playing the odds. Family members—primarily noncustodial parents—were involved in the majority of child kidnappings. And from what little Cooper had revealed during their brief discussion the night before, Kristen had gleaned that Norah Cabot Cooper hadn't seen her daughter in nearly three years.

She was in the middle of dressing around 7:00 a.m. when her cell phone rang. Stepping into a pair of brown trousers, she grabbed the phone. "Tandy."

"Sam Cooper here."

Her feet got tangled in the trousers and she stumbled onto the bed, hitting it heavily. "Mr. Cooper." She'd given him her business card, with her cell phone number, but he was the last person she'd expected to hear from this morning. "Has something happened?"

"I'm not sure," he said. "Maybe."

She tucked the phone between her chin and shoulder and finished pulling on her pants. "Maybe?"

"My secretary called from my office in Birmingham. She got in early today and found a package for me sitting in front of my office door."

"What kind of package?" Visions of mail bombs flitted through her head. Maybe an anthrax letter. Cooper was a county prosecutor, almost as good a target as a judge or a politician.

"No return address. No postal mark. Right now building security is examining it, and if they think it's a threat, they'll call the cops. But I thought you'd want to know." Sam sounded tired. She doubted he'd managed even as much sleep as she had. "I should probably go into the office, but—"

"No, stay with your kid. If it turns out to be anything we need to worry about, I'll handle it."

There was a pause on the other end of the phone. "I don't want this case mucked up by police agencies marking territory."

If that was a warning, she could hardly blame him. She'd seen her share of interagency wrangling during her seven years as a police officer. "I'll call your office when I get to work, and if I think the package is remotely connected to this case, I'll go to Birmingham and sort it out myself."

"Thank you." After a brief pause he added, "Maddy liked you. You made her feel safer last night when you talked to her. I know that was probably hard on you, considering—you know."

Her heart sank. So he did know who she was. Everybody in Gossamer Ridge knew. Oh, well, the brief anonymity had been nice while it lasted. "It's my job," she said gruffly.

"Thank you anyway." He rang off.

Kristen closed her phone and released a long breath. He was right. It had been hard dealing with Maddy. Kids in general, really. The psychiatrists had all assured her the prickly, uncomfortable feeling she had around young children would go away eventually, as her memories of that horrible day faded with distance.

Only they hadn't faded. The pain had receded, even most of the fear, but not those last, wretched memories of her brothers and sisters.

Their last moments on earth.

She arrived at work in a gloomy mood and found Foley sitting at her desk, jotting a note. He looked up with a half smile. "Ah, I was about to leave you a note. One of Sam Cooper's neighbors called, said she might have seen someone suspicious lurking around the Cooper house earlier in the evening. I thought I'd go hear her out. Let's go."

"Let me make a phone call first." As she looked up the number for the Jefferson County District Attorney's office, she told Foley about Sam Cooper's call. He arched an eyebrow but didn't speak while she waited for someone to pick up. After several rings, voice mail picked up.

"Maybe they've cleared the building, just in case?"

Kristen left a brief message, then dialed Sam Cooper's cell phone number.

He answered on the first ring. "Detective Tandy?"

"I got voice mail when I called your office."

"I know. I managed to get a colleague on his cell. They've evacuated the building and the bomb squad is examining the package. Tim promised to call me back as soon as he knew something more, but this waiting is driving me nuts."

"I'll drive down to Birmingham and check it out for you."

"I'll meet you there."

"Shouldn't you stay with your daughter?"

"Jake and Gabe took her and my nephew Mike fishing to keep their minds off what's going on with Cissy. They'll be out on the lake all morning."

"You should've gone with them."

His soft laugh was humorless. "I'd be on the phone the whole time anyway."

"Then why don't you ride along with me?" Kristen supposed he might be of use to her if the Birmingham Police didn't want to play nice.

"Okay," he agreed. "Do you know where Cooper Marina is?"

"Yeah. See you in fifteen minutes."

KRISTEN TANDY'S CHEVROLET pulled into the marina parking lot with a minute to spare. Sam didn't wait for her to get out. "Where's Detective Foley?" he asked as he slid into the passenger seat.

She cranked the engine. "Talking to a neighbor of yours. Might be a lead." She didn't sound convinced.

"I talked to my colleague again just before you arrived." Sam buckled in as she headed toward the main highway. "Bomb squad's still inside. Nobody seems to know anything yet."

"Don't imagine it's a job you'd want to rush."

He slanted a look at her. Her eyes were on the narrow road twisting through the woods from his parents' marina to the two-lane highway leading into town, her lips curved in a wry smile. He'd been too preoccupied last night to really process much about her, like the fact that she was strikingly pretty. He'd been right about how young she was, though. No older than her late twenties.

She'd shed her jacket to drive, a well-cut white blouse revealing soft curves her boxy business suit had hidden the night before. In the morning sunlight, her skin was as smooth and pale as fine porcelain and her sleek blond hair shimmered like gold. He was surprised by how attractive he found her, under the circumstances.

He distracted himself with a question. "You haven't been a detective long, have you?"

Her expression grew defensive. "Six months."

He nodded. "Big case for you, I guess."

"Not my usual petty theft or meth lab," she admitted.

"How about Foley? How long has he been a detective?"

Her gaze cut toward him. "Should we send you our résumés?"

"Would you?" he countered, more to see her reaction than any real doubt about their credentials.

She took a swift breath through her nose. He could almost hear her mentally counting to ten, he thought, stifling a grin. "Detective Foley has been an investigator for ten years. Five of those were with the Memphis Police Department Homicide Bureau. I've been an officer with the Gossamer Ridge Police Department since I turned twenty-one."

He couldn't hold back a smile. "That long, huh?"

She slanted him an exasperated look, her eyes spitting blue fire. "Anything new with your niece? Last time I checked, the hospital said there was no change."

"That's because there's not been any change," he said, his smile fading. "Better than a downturn, I suppose, but a little good news would be welcome."

"Have they diagnosed the problem?"

"She has a skull fracture and some minor bleeding in her brain. Right now they think she's got a good chance of full recovery, but I think that's based on her age and relative health more than anything they're seeing in the CAT scans."

"Damn. We could really use her statement."

He shot her a look.

Her neck reddened and her lips pressed into a tight line. "Sorry. I'm still working on my self-edit button."

"You're right," he admitted. "We could use her statement."

"I checked in with the lab before I left the station. They're comparing all the fingerprints to eliminate the ones you'd expect to find, so it's going to take time to see if there are any unidentified prints." She turned onto the interstate on-ramp, heading south to Birmingham. "I know you said last night you didn't think your ex could be a suspect—"

"She doesn't have a motive," he said bluntly. "She ended our marriage as much because she didn't want to be a mother as because she didn't want to be married to me. Maddy was an accident she couldn't deal with." He clamped his mouth shut before more bitter words escaped.

"Some women just aren't mother material," Kristen murmured.

"Some women don't even try," he shot back.

She was silent for a moment, a muscle in her jaw working. After a bit, she said, "Maybe when we get to Birmingham, we'll have the answer to who's behind the attack on your niece."

"Maybe." He doubted it, though. It wasn't likely that the guy who broke into his house, nearly killed his niece and tried to kidnap his daughter would send Sam a package that could be traced back to him.

Within thirty minutes they pulled up to the police cordon blocking traffic in front of the Jefferson County District Attorney's office. Sam directed Kristen to park in the deck across from the county courthouse, and they walked down the street to where the police had set up the barriers.

Sam spotted Tim Melton, the colleague he'd reached earlier. He crossed to Melton's side. "Any news?"

"I just saw someone from the bomb squad come out and talk to Captain Rayburn," Tim answered. He gave Kristen Tandy a curious look. "Tim Melton," he introduced himself.

"Detective Tandy," she answered.

"Oh. Right." He looked back at Sam. "How's your niece?"

"No change," he answered tersely. "Detective Tandy's investigating the case."

"I guess that package might be connected?"

"Maybe. We'll see." Kristen stepped closer to the police tape. "Any way to get me in there?" she asked Sam.

He searched the crowd of policemen and firefighters on the other side of the cordon to see if he could catch the eye of one of the handful of officers he knew by name. A few seconds later, a sandy-haired detective named Cropwell spotted him and crossed to the tape to greet him.

"Nothing like fan mail, huh?" he said with a bleak grin.

"What's the latest?"

"Perkins from the Bomb Squad said they've x-rayed it and don't think it's a bomb. They were about to open it last I heard." Cropwell glanced over his shoulder. "Rayburn'll probably be the first to know."

Kristen Tandy flipped open a slim leather wallet, displaying her badge. Sam had a feeling that Cropwell wouldn't exactly be impressed—Gossamer Ridge was small potatoes as Alabama towns went—but he had to admire her bravado.

"Kristen Tandy, Gossamer Ridge Police Department. We believe the package delivered to Mr. Cooper's office may be connected to a home invasion case we're investigating."

As Sam had expected, Cropwell looked at Kristen's badge with a mixture of amusement and disdain. "We'll let you know if anything in the package is of concern to you, Detective."

"Detective Tandy is investigating an attack on my niece, who was caring for my daughter at the time," Sam said firmly. "If this is connected, I want her in on it."

Kristen didn't drop her gaze from Cropwell's, but Sam saw her expression shift slightly, a slight curve of her pink lips in response to his defense.

Cropwell looked at Sam, instantly apologetic. "Yes, sir."

"May I enter the scene?" Kristen asked, her voice tinted with long-suffering patience that made Cropwell flush.

"Yeah, fine." He lifted the cordon and let Kristen come under. But when Sam started to follow, he blocked entrance. "Sorry, sir," he said, his eyes glittering with payback, "but civilians aren't allowed behind the tape. Not even you, sir."

Sam nodded, acknowledging Cropwell's small victory.

Kristen would have died rather than let it show, but mingling with the Birmingham police officers busy outside the Jefferson County District Attorney's office was beginning to make her feel like the biggest rube that ever walked a city street. It wasn't that they treated her badly; most of the other policemen on the scene were polite and helpful, answering her questions and helping her get caught up as quickly as possible. But she was clearly the youngest detective there, and she could tell from the wary gazes of some of the Birmingham detectives that she'd still be wearing a uniform and driving patrol if she weren't on some hayseed rural police force.

She was waiting with the other detectives for word from the bomb squad when her cell phone rang. She excused herself, walked a few feet away and answered. "Tandy."

"I hear you're in Birmingham." Her boss's familiar voice rumbled over the phone, tinged with the same frustrated affection Carl usually showed when it came to her.

"Why do I feel like I just violated curfew?" she murmured.

"Got anything yet?"

"We're waiting for word from the bomb squad. All we really know so far is that there's not actually a bomb in the package."

"That's progress, I suppose."

"Heard anything from Foley? Did he get anything out of the interview with Cooper's neighbor?"

"A rough description of a blue van she saw circling the neighborhood a few times earlier in the day, but nothing concrete. Foley's taking her some pictures to look at, see if she can pick out a make and model but right now, he's going door to door, talking to other neighbors."

She didn't miss the slight tone of admonishment. "And you think I should be there doing that instead of being here waiting for news from the Birmingham bomb squad?"

"You said it, not me."

"You said it without saying it." Movement to her left caught her attention. "Bomb squad's coming out. Gotta go."

She rang off and returned to the queue of police officers waiting for word. A tall, sandy-haired squad member peeled away from the rest of the group and moved toward the detectives. He carried a clear plastic bag containing what appeared to be the remains of a large manila envelope.

"No bomb, no foreign substances. You're clear to examine it," he told a tall, barrel-chested man standing near the front of the line. Kristen dug in her memory for the detective's name. Raymond—

no, Rayburn. Captain Rayburn. She took advantage of her small size to slip through the huddle and reach Rayburn's side just as he donned a pair of latex gloves and carefully opened the plastic bag.

He slanted a look toward her, his expression hard to read for a moment. Then his features relaxed and he gave a little half nod, as if beckoning her closer. "Reckon you'll want to see this, too, Detective."

She scooted closer. The contents were, indeed, the remains of a manila envelope. The bomb squad had apparently used a razor knife to slice it open and examine the contents.

Captain Rayburn reached into the plastic bag and delicately opened the edges of the envelope. Inside lay what looked like a small stack of five-by-seven photographs. Careful to touch only the outer edges, Rayburn pulled the stack from the envelope.

Kristen's heart plummeted.

The top photo was an image of a little girl dressed in a robin's-egg-blue shorts set, swinging on a swing at Gossamer Park.

The girl was Maddy Cooper.

Chapter Three

Sam stared at the photographs, his stomach rebelling. There were twelve in total, five-by-sevens taken on a digital camera according to the lab tech who examined them first before releasing them back to the Birmingham detectives. Each photo depicted his daughter Maddy at play, in a variety of places, from the playground at Gossamer Park to the farmer's market on Main Street. Once or twice Sam was in the photo, as well; another time, his parents. One photo featured Maddy with Sam's sister Hannah, fishing from one of the marina's fishing piers. Maddy was holding up a small crappie and grinning at her aunt.

He looked away from the photos and rubbed his eyes. They felt full of grit.

"I called my office." Kristen Tandy's voice was toneless. He looked up at her and found her gaze fixed on the photos. "Foley's on his way to the marina now to let your parents know what's going on."

"I need to get back there."

Kristen nodded. "The detectives have agreed to send me scans of these photos." She looked up at Dave Rayburn, who gave her a nod. She and the captain seemed to have come to an understanding, Sam noted.

"So we can go now?"

"Yeah." Kristen shook hands with Rayburn and led Sam out of the office.

They didn't talk on the way to the car. Sam wasn't even sure what to say. The very notion of someone stalking his baby girl was so surreal, he spent half the drive back to Gossamer Ridge wondering if he was stuck in a nightmare.

Kristen broke the silence they'd maintained to that point, her voice uncharacteristically warm. "We're going to find the son of a bitch who took those pictures."

He looked at her. Her gaze angled forward, eyes on the road, her jaw set like stone. "He dropped them off yesterday evening," he said aloud. "Before he even tried to take her. He wanted that to be the first thing I saw the morning I woke up with my daughter gone." And he'd been sneaky, too, leaving the package outside the building after hours—but before the receptionist had left for the day. He'd probably waited around to make sure she saw the package and took it back to the office before she finished locking up for the night.

Kristen looked at him then, just a quick glance,

but he saw fiery anger flashing in her blue eyes. "It doesn't matter that the security cameras didn't catch him. It won't stop us."

He hoped she was right.

At the marina, Kristen parked beside the bait shop, next to a Chevy Impala identical to the one she was driving. "Foley," she said to Sam as they got out of the car.

Inside the bait shop, Maddy sat on her grandfather's knee playing with a large cork bobber, tossing it in the air like a ball and nearly tumbling off Mike Cooper's knees trying to catch it. Nearby, Foley stood at the counter, talking in low tones with Sam's mother. All four of them looked up as Sam and Kristen entered.

Maddy's eyes lit up and she scrambled down from Mike's lap. "Miss Kristen!" she squealed, beaming up at Kristen Tandy as she ran to greet them.

Sam felt Kristen stiffen beside him. He quickly intercepted his boisterous daughter before she flung herself at Kristen's knees and hoisted her into his arms. "What? No hello for your daddy?"

"Hi, Daddy!" She patted his face affectionately before twisting in his arms to look at Kristen. "Daddy Mike's gonna let me feed the worms, Miss Kristen. D'you wanna come with us?"

Kristen looked positively green, but Sam suspected it had nothing to do with the prospect of feeding worms.

He tamped down a bit of resentment. "Miss Kristen has a job to do, baby. And I'm afraid you and Daddy Mike are gonna have to go worm feeding some other day. I've got plans for us this afternoon. Want to know what?"

"What?" She caught his face between her hands again, making his heart swell. But instead of her lopsided grin, he saw static, candid images captured in a series of still photographs. He glanced at Kristen, who was watching him, her expression for once unguarded. The look on her face was utter devastation. There was no other word for it.

He cleared his throat and looked back at Maddy. "We're going to have a movie marathon! All the princesses—as many as we can get through before bedtime."

Maddy wriggled excitedly in his arms. "Really?"

"Really."

Sam heard Detective Foley make a low, sympathetic sound behind him. Normally, Sam would agree—an afternoon and evening full of animated fairy-tale musicals were to be avoided at all costs. But this time, he could think of nowhere he'd rather be than his parents' guest cottage with his little girl tucked safely against him on the sofa, miraculously still with him to watch dancing brooms and singing mice.

"Can Miss Kristen come, too?" Maddy asked.

"I told you, Miss Kristen has to work."

"But after work, can she come, too?"

Sam started to say no, but Kristen cleared her throat behind him. "Yeah, Maddy. I can come after work."

Sam looked up at Kristen, startled. She met his gaze, sheer terror shining in her blue eyes. But her small, pointed chin jutted forward, like a soldier preparing for battle.

"Are you sure?" he asked.

"Yes," she said, unconvincingly. "Y'all are staying here for a few days, right?"

He started to tell her it wasn't a good idea, but the glee in Maddy's laughter stopped him before he uttered a word. He looked at his daughter, finding her grinning at Kristen with sheer delight, and stayed silent. "Yeah. There's a guest cottage down the hill from my folks' place."

"I can be there by seven-thirty," Kristen told him quietly after Maddy had climbed down to follow her grandfather into the back room. "I'll bring some microwave popcorn or something."

"You don't have to do this." Sam didn't miss the reluctance in her eyes.

"She goes to sleep—what? Eight? Eight-thirty?"

"Yeah," Sam agreed, not following.

"Good. Then you and I can go over a few things."

He arched an eyebrow. "A few things?"

"A few cases, actually." She stepped away from the counter, lowering her voice. "I think whoever sent you those photos may be someone you've crossed in your work. You were a prosecutor before you moved back here to Alabama, weren't you?"

"Yeah, I was an assistant Commonwealth's Attorney in Arlington County."

"Tried a few cases?"

"You think someone I prosecuted is looking for revenge?"

She shrugged. "It's worth thinking about, isn't it?"

"Okay, I'll think about it." He shot her a wary grin. "Something to do while the princesses are singing."

Her answering smile transformed her face briefly, giving him a glimpse of what she might have looked like had her tragic past not left indelible traces on her young features. Her eyes shimmered like a cloudless sky reflected in a calm lake, and the worry lines creasing her forehead disappeared as if erased.

He felt another unexpected tug of attraction, sudden and primitive, that lingered even after her smile faded into the care-worn lines he'd become accustomed to. He cleared his throat as Maddy and his father reemerged from the back room with the bait containers. "Okay, we'll see you around seven-thirty."

"Foley, I'm heading into the office to type up my report. You coming?"

"Uh, yeah." Foley's gaze moved quickly from her to Sam and back again. "Call us if you need us." He fell in step with Kristen as she headed for the exit.

"Bye, Miss Kristen!" Maddy called from behind the counter.

Kristen lifted her hand to Maddy, shot Sam an enigmatic look and left the bait shop, Foley on her heels.

"She seems like a nice girl," Beth Cooper commented, patting Sam's back as she passed on her way back to the front counter. "Too sad about what happened with her mama."

Sam dragged his gaze away from the empty doorway. "I know the basics—her mother killed her brothers and sisters and tried to kill her. But what else do you recall about it?"

His mother gave him an odd look. "That's pretty much all I remember. The news reports at the time were vague."

"What happened to the mother?"

"I don't think she went to jail. I want to say maybe the state mental hospital or something like that." Beth's gaze was quizzical. "You're awfully interested in Detective Tandy all of a sudden."

"Stop it, Mom."

Her smile faded. "Just be careful, okay? Maddy's at a ripe age to get attached to a woman in your life. She's old enough to wonder why her mother doesn't ever come around."

He'd bent over backward to make excuses for Norah to Maddy, more for his daughter's sake than his ex-wife's. But Maddy was nearing school age, and she'd soon start wondering why everyone else in her class had a mommy to take care of them. One day his excuses wouldn't be enough.

One day, he'd have to explain that not all mommies wanted to be mommies, and there was nothing she could have said or done or been to make a difference. It was going to be the hardest thing he'd ever done in his life.

No point in making it harder by letting another woman so clearly not cut out for motherhood break his daughter's heart.

"YOU CAN'T BE SERIOUS." Kristen stared at Carl Madison, shaking her head. "Carl, there's got to be someone else—"

"I could find someone else," the captain of detectives conceded. "But Foley says the child already likes and trusts you. And honestly? You need to do it for yourself."

"Don't do that." Kristen glared at her foster father, her anger festering. "You're not my father anymore."

"You never let me be," he said bleakly.

Guilt stoked her anger. "All I ever wanted was to be left alone to get on with my life. That's still all I want."

"You're not getting on with your life. You're hiding behind your badge and your attitude, avoiding anything that scares you or challenges you. I'm not talking to you as a father now," he added when she opened her mouth to protest. "I'm your boss, and this is a job I think you can do if you put your mind to it. Are you telling me I'm wrong?"

Nostrils flaring, Kristen looked away from Carl. "I don't think Sam Cooper will agree to it."

"I think he'll agree to anything that will keep his daughter safe from another attack." Carl's voice dipped an octave. "Fathers are like that."

Kristen stood up, her legs trembling with pent-up anger and a healthy dose of apprehension. "It's a terrible idea."

"But you'll do it?"

"I don't have a choice, do I?" She left his office, giving the door an extra-hard push as she shut it behind her. The slam echoed down the corridor behind her.

Foley looked up as she entered the bull pen, making a face at the sight of her scowl. "Good afternoon to you, too."

"Carl wants me on full-time babysitting duty with Maddy Cooper," she growled.

Foley's eyebrows lifted. "Really? I was betting he'd tell you not to go on your movie-night date with Sam Cooper."

She shot him a dark glare. "It's an informal interview with a crime victim at his home."

"Over popcorn and movies."

"The popcorn and *princess* movies are for the kid." Kristen crossed to her desk, grabbed her purse and headed for the door before he asked more questions.

"That kid's got a thing for you," Foley said as she passed.

"Then maybe she'll remember something new and tell it to her new best buddy," she retorted.

"That's not fair, Tandy. And you're not that cold."

She stopped in the doorway and turned back to look at him. "I have to be that cold, don't I? Especially if I'm going to be Maddy's best friend 24/7."

Foley shook his head. "I don't think that's what Carl had in mind. I know Sam Cooper won't put up with it."

She sighed, leaning against the doorjamb. "What am I supposed to do? Blow off the assignment? Do you really believe there's not going to be another attempt to grab that kid?"

"No. I think someone brazen enough to send photos to her daddy is brazen enough to try to snatch her again," Foley conceded. "But I've seen you with kids. You look like you're allergic. I keep waiting for you to break out in hives."

She pushed away from the door frame and swung her hair over her shoulder. "I'm not good with kids."

Foley's expression was full of pity. "It's not that you're not good with them, Tandy. You're afraid of them." When she didn't answer him, he added, "Are you going to do what Madison wants?"

She left without answering, her chest tight with dread.

"LET'S GET SOMETHING straight," Sam murmured to Kristen an hour later after Maddy had squeezed out from between them to go to the bathroom. "Clearly, you're not the maternal type."

Kristen's eyes met his. The vulnerability that flashed there for a moment stunned him, but it disappeared quickly, leaving her expression unreadable. "No, I'm not."

"Then, I think from now on, we should limit your interactions with Maddy to formal visits."

Her gaze remained steady, but Sam saw a flicker of something in the depths of her blue eyes that might have been pain. Again, it slipped away as quickly as it had come. "I was afraid you'd say that," she murmured. "But—"

Maddy came back into the room and bounced onto the sofa between them. "Unpause!" she said brightly to her father.

Sam hit Play and the syrupy strains of a princess love theme filled the room, ending the conversation with Kristen for the moment. But Sam felt her gaze on his face, sensed the tension buzzing around them, as whatever it was she'd started to tell him lingered, unsaid but unforgotten.

Within an hour, Maddy's eyes began to droop, and she gave only a halfhearted protest when Sam finally stopped the DVD player and carried her off to bed. He lingered a few moments as she tossed and turned, still not used to the strange bed. She demanded a story, and he complied with a quick reading of *Horton Hears a Who*. She was asleep within a couple of minutes.

Sam put the book on the nightstand and tucked her in, lingering a moment to run his fingers over the satiny curve of her round cheek. Swaddled in the enormous old wedding ring quilt that had belonged to his grandmother, she looked tiny. So very fragile and breakable.

He felt rather than heard Kristen enter the room behind him. He turned to find her standing in the doorway, her narrow-eyed gaze fixed on his daughter as if looking for something in Maddy's soft features. Tonight she wore a pale green T-shirt and jeans, her hair loose and a little wild, very different from the buttoned-up police detective he'd spent the morning with. The T-shirt revealed even more new curves he hadn't seen before, and the snug jeans made her legs look miles long.

His whole body tightened pleasantly in response.

Kristen stepped out into the hallway, and he rose to follow, closing the door to the bedroom behind him. She faced him as they reached the living room, her tense expression working hard to kill the light sexual buzz he'd been enjoying.

"I have something to ask you." Her voice was tight, as if she'd had to force the words from her throat.

He grew instantly apprehensive. "What?"

"Carl—Captain Madison—believes there's a strong likelihood that whoever broke into your home is going to go after Maddy again. I agree with him."

"So do I," Sam conceded, though her stark assessment made his stomach hurt.

"He wants to assign someone to Maddy full-time."

Sam frowned. "Full-time? Like a bodyguard?"

"Yes."

Sam stepped away from her, rubbing his jaw. His beard stubble scraped his palm with a rasping sound. "I don't know if she'll take to some stranger coming in to play nanny—"

"It won't be a stranger," Kristen said, her voice even tighter than before.

Tension stretched in the air between them as he slowly turned to look at her, understanding dawning. Her eyes locked with his, wide and scared.

"I'll be Maddy's bodyguard," she said.

Chapter Four

Waiting for Sam to break his stunned silence, Kristen didn't know whether she wanted him to agree or refuse. On a purely visceral level, anything that saved her from spending every day and night with Maddy Cooper would be a welcome response. But it was also a coward's choice.

She wasn't a coward, no matter what Foley or Carl thought.

"That's the last thing I expected you to say." Sam sat down on the sofa and passed his hand over his jaw. His palm made a raspy noise against his beard stubble, and she was surprised to feel a flutter of feminine awareness in her belly.

He was an attractive man. Not handsome exactly, not by Hollywood standards. His appeal was edgier— raw male power, evident in the broad expanse of his shoulders and the lean, almost feral features that even a veneer of civilization couldn't temper.

She sat beside him, ignoring the tremble in her knees. "It wasn't my idea."

He shot her a dark look. "You don't say."

"That doesn't mean it's the wrong thing to do," she continued, ignoring his sarcasm. "Maddy may be in further danger, and I'm the best person, under the circumstances, to protect her. She seems to like and trust me. I will do anything in my power to protect her."

"My brother could do the same thing."

"He's on special assignment with the Drug Enforcement Agency. You know that." She had checked into Aaron Cooper's availability herself, during the short hour between Carl's order and her arrival at the Cooper family guesthouse.

"My sister's husband is also a deputy."

"Riley Patterson? The one who's currently in Arizona for his parents' fortieth wedding anniversary?"

"You did a background check on my whole family?"

She had, in fact. A cursory one, anyway. Standard operating procedure for child abduction cases. "He and your sister won't be back until Monday."

Sam frowned at her, his gaze intense. She could see him weighing all the ramifications in his mind as he stared her down. Could he trust her with his daughter?

Should he?

She withstood his scrutiny for as long as she could before finally blurting, "Yes or no?"

His nostrils flared briefly. "Okay. There's an

extra bedroom you can use. But I don't want our lives disrupted any more than they have to be. Maddy still gets to visit with my parents and go fishing with Jake and Gabe. Understood? If I say she's safe with someone without you there you don't interfere."

Kristen nodded. The less time she had to spend alone with Maddy, the better. "I know you're probably wary about bringing a gun in here with Maddy around—"

Sam's lips curved into a grim smile. "I'm armed myself, Detective Tandy."

The deadly serious tone of his voice made Kristen's stomach tighten. So she'd been right to see the masculinity beneath the well-cut suits and expensive ties. Despite the Italian silk and the fancy letters at the end of his name, Sam Cooper had grown up here in the hills of Chickasaw County and hardened his native strength with a stint in the Marine Corps.

She paid back his earlier scrutiny by indulging herself with a long, appraising look, smiling as he reacted to the tit for tat with a look of grudging amusement. She knew Sam Cooper had graduated from law school and passed the bar exam by the young age of twenty-four and spent the next five years working as a JAG lawyer before taking a civilian job in the District of Columbia. Sure, it hadn't been a combat assignment, but everybody in the Marine Corps had to go through boot camp, didn't they?

If the hard muscles and flat planes she glimpsed beneath his olive-green T-shirt and faded jeans were anything to go by, he'd kept up with the fitness regimen even after he'd left the service. She looked away.

"I keep wondering who'd do something like this." The vulnerability in Sam's voice caught her by surprise. "I'm not rich. I'm not a celebrity. I don't think I could scrape up a ransom payment if I tried."

"I think maybe revenge," she offered quietly. The haggard look in his eyes suggested that answer had been squirming around the back of his mind since the attempted kidnapping. "Or some other personal agenda," she added.

His eyes narrowed. "You're still thinking about my ex."

"The majority of child abductions are familial. You have full custody of Maddy and moved her to another state recently—"

"With Norah's blessing," Sam said firmly. "She's welcome to see Maddy whenever she likes. She chooses not to."

"Why not?"

Sam's lips narrowed to a thin line. His gaze shifted toward the hallway, as if he was afraid Maddy might overhear. He nodded toward the cottage's kitchen nook, leading the way. When he spoke, he kept his voice low. "She didn't want to have Maddy in the first place. The pregnancy wasn't planned. I talked her into the marriage."

Kristen felt a cold tingle crawl up her spine. "She didn't want to have children at all?"

He flashed a bleak smile. "No. But she knew how much I did. So she agreed to marry me and have the baby, give the whole wedded bliss thing a shot." He nudged a folded dishrag across the counter with one long finger. "Didn't work out."

"How long did it last?"

"Nine months, until Maddy was three months old."

Not very long to give marriage and motherhood a chance, she thought. "And she gave you full custody?"

"Since our divorce was all about getting out of playing mommy and wife, yeah. She did."

Kristen wasn't sure how to respond. There had been a time in her life when she couldn't imagine how a woman could turn her back on her child. But that was a long time ago, before she'd seen firsthand what a mother was capable of doing to her children. She cleared her throat. "Some women just aren't meant to be mothers."

When she dared to look at him again, she was shocked to find his expression sympathetic. She'd expected disgust.

She hardened herself against the compassion in his warm blue eyes. "I looked into your ex anyway. She's just become engaged. Did you know that?"

He looked surprised. "More background checks, Detective?"

So he didn't know about the engagement. Interesting.

"Who's she marrying?" he asked, almost as an afterthought. She wasn't sure if he was indifferent or just pretending to be.

"Graham Stilson," she answered.

One dark eyebrow notched upward. "Junior or Senior?"

"Junior. Do you know him?"

Sam turned to face her fully, resting his elbows on the narrow breakfast bar behind him. "Stilson Junior was a trial lawyer in the D.C. area before he was elected to the state senate. We crossed paths now and then. I know his father better, though. Stilson Senior is a judge."

Clearly, he didn't care much for Stilson Junior. Kristen wondered how much of his dislike was wrapped up in unresolved feelings for his ex, annoyed with herself for her curiosity. What had she expected, that he'd have lost all interest in a woman he'd once loved enough to marry?

Not that Sam Cooper's feelings were of any importance, she reminded herself. It was his ex-wife who was currently on Kristen's suspect list, not Sam.

"I asked her assistant to track her down and have her call me. Nothing yet," she said aloud.

"Norah doesn't get motivated to return calls unless she thinks you can do something for her," Sam said with a shrug. "I left a message for her, too."

"I thought you said you didn't think she was a suspect."

"I don't," he said firmly. "But she's Maddy's mom. She should know what's going on."

Would Norah Cabot even care? She hadn't given much thought to her daughter's life so far—why would she start now?

Sam might not be indifferent to his ex-wife, but he clearly resented her abandonment of their child, and on a surface level, Kristen knew she should find Norah Cabot's actions selfish, as well. But her own mother had had no business raising children. Kristen had seen the horrible consequences. As far as she was concerned, Maddy was lucky. She had a daddy to love and protect her, and she didn't have to deal with her indifferent mother at all.

How much different would Kristen's own life have been if she'd had a father around to make sure she and her brothers and sisters were safe and cared for?

Sam interrupted her dark thoughts. "I had my office e-mail me the felony cases I've worked on since I took the job a few months ago. There are only five—they gave me a light load until I could get my bearings. I've printed them out, if you want to take a look tonight. We can see if there's anything in those files that might have set someone off."

Following him back to the sitting area, she kicked herself for not having asked him about his current case files sooner. She was letting her kid phobia take over this whole case.

Time to cowboy up. If she couldn't handle one four-year-old poppet—and her sexy grouch of a father—her career was in serious trouble.

SAM SAT BACK AN HOUR LATER, rubbing his eyes. He'd read through all five cases and saw nothing he could imagine enraging someone enough to come after his child. "What if this isn't about me?" he asked Kristen.

She looked up from the case file she was reading. "Just some random kidnapper stalking Maddy? For what purpose?"

His stomach recoiled at the only answer that made sense. "A pedophile?"

She shook her head. "This doesn't fit a pedophile's M.O. They're cowards. They like targets of opportunity."

"That guy in Utah broke into his target's house and took her out of her bedroom," he reminded her.

"That's rare."

"But not impossible."

She wrinkled her brow at him. "Do you want it to be a pedophile?" she asked pointedly.

"God, no!" The thought was horrifying.

Her expression gentled. "Whatever pushed this guy's buttons, it's not your fault."

How could she know that? What if he'd done something, said something or forgotten something that had set the kidnapper off? What if this whole thing was about payback?

What if he'd been the one who'd put his daughter at risk?

Kristen's hand stole across the sofa and curled around his, her grip tight. The touch felt like a jolt of electricity, setting his whole body abuzz, and he was caught off guard by a flood of pure male attraction.

He'd always gone for high-octane women like Norah Cabot, with her expensive French perfume and her designer shoes. He'd worked with many beautiful, even glamorous women, and he'd always found them exciting and sexy. He'd just figured that kind of woman was his type.

So why was this quiet, no-nonsense, small-town cop making his blood run hot in a way it hadn't in years?

She let go of his hand and looked down at the files spread across the coffee table. "We should look at some of your case files from D.C. Can you get your hands on those?"

His fingers still tingled from her touch. He closed his fist and cleared his throat. "Probably more red tape than we'd like. I'll help you set that into motion. However, I keep a detailed log of all my cases—the major figures involved, whether the outcome was a conviction, an acquittal or a plea bargain, that kind of thing. It's in one of the storage boxes at home. I'll stop by and get the log, and we can go through it, as well."

"Could you get it tomorrow?"

"If you're okay with being here alone with Maddy," he said, watching her carefully for her reaction.

The line of her lips tightened a little, but she gave a nod. "Of course. It's my job."

He wasn't sure if she was reassuring him or herself. He could tell she still had doubts. He dropped his gaze to the back of Kristen's hand, where a white burn scar still marred the skin. Had she seen her mother kill her brothers and sister, or had she stumbled upon the aftermath?

Did it even matter which? Both would have been horrific.

Kristen's eyes flickered up to meet his, as if the sudden silence between them made her nervous. He felt a rush of pity he couldn't quite hide, and her expression shifted from vulnerability to a hard, cool mask of indifference. She edged away from him, readying herself to stand. "It's getting late," she began. "I need to go home and pack for tomorrow."

His cell phone interrupted, the shrill sound jolting his spine like an electric shock. He fished it from his pocket. The display showed an area code he didn't recognize.

"Cooper," he answered, slanting a quick look at Kristen, who sat very still, watching him.

A low, vibrant voice greeted him. "Hi, Sam. It's me."

Norah. He'd left a message for her to call, but he hadn't expected to hear from her tonight. "Thanks for calling back."

Kristen gave him a curious look, but before he could tell her who was on the other line, the bedroom door opened and Maddy stumbled out, her hair wild and her eyes damp with tears.

"Daddy?" she mewled.

Torn between dealing with Norah and comforting his daughter, Sam shot Kristen a pleading look. For a second, her eyes widened and she looked ready to bolt, but she regained control quickly and crossed to Maddy's side.

"Sam, are you there?" Norah's voice drew his attention back to the phone.

Sam watched Kristen crouch by Maddy and begin talking to her in a soft tone. "Yeah, I'm here. Sorry. Maddy woke up."

"Your message said you had something important to tell me." He heard a hint of impatience in Norah's voice, probably because he'd mentioned Maddy. She didn't like to hear about Maddy. Must be easier to believe she did the right thing when she didn't have to think about a little girl growing up without her mommy.

Too bad. What he had to tell her had everything to do with Maddy. And this time, she was going to listen.

KRISTEN COAXED MADDY BACK into the bedroom, though she wished she could stay and listen to Sam's end of the conversation. He hadn't said the caller was his ex-wife, but Kristen could tell from his defensive body language and the immediate tension in his voice that he was talking to someone with the power to hurt him. She assumed Norah Cabot was such a person.

"Can you read me a story?" Maddy asked.

Kristen looked at the sleepy little face staring up at her from the pillows and her heart shattered. She struggled to stay focused, to keep her mind in the present as it began to wander helplessly into the nightmarish past.

Read the little girl a book, Kristen. You can do that.

She picked up the book lying on the small bedside table. Dr. Seuss. Her heart squeezed.

Seuss had been Julie's favorite. Kristen had read *Green Eggs and Ham* so often she had it memorized. Sometimes, usually late at night when she was tired and couldn't fight off the memories, the rhymes and rhythms of the child's book flitted through her mind, interspersed with the image of Julie's limp body lying at the foot of her blood-stained bed.

Kristen closed her eyes and took a deep breath, clutching the book against her chest.

"Can't you read, Miss Kristen?"

Her eyes snapped open. Maddy Cooper gazed up at her with wide green eyes full of sweet sympathy.

"I can read it for you," Maddy added, patting the bed beside her in invitation.

Kristen stared at the tiny hand thumping lightly on the pale pink sheet. Another image of Julie fluttered through her mind, surprisingly sweet. Like

Maddy, her little sister had also owned a favorite pair of pajamas—bright yellow with black stripes, inspiring Kristen to nickname her Julie Bee. Julie used to "read" to Kristen, too, flipping through the pages as she recited her favorite books by memory.

Blinking back the tears burning her eyes, Kristen sat beside Maddy, releasing a pent-up breath.

The little girl edged closer, her body warm and compact against Kristen's side. She took the Dr. Seuss book from Kristen's nerveless fingers and flipped to the first page, where Horton the elephant sat in a bright blue pool, happily splashing himself with water.

As Maddy began to recite the familiar story in her childish lisp, Kristen closed her eyes and relaxed, not fighting the flood of sweet memories washing over her.

Julie had been an adorable baby, the youngest of the five Tandy kids and the one Kristen had reared almost single-handedly as her mother's break with reality had widened those last few years. Kristen hadn't shared a father with her two youngest siblings, but she hadn't cared. Her own father was long gone, and neither of the men who'd fathered baby Julie and six-year-old Kevin had stuck around long enough to see them born. It was just Kristen, the younger kids and their mother, and for most of Kristen's memory, her mother had been undependable.

Realizing Maddy had fallen silent, Kristen

opened her eyes and found the little girl gazing up at her with solemn green eyes. "Don't cry, Miss Kristen." She patted Kristen's arm. "Horton will find the clover. You'll see."

Kristen dashed away the tears, forcing a smile, even as she struggled to hold back a stream of darker memories. She hadn't had a sweet thought about her brothers and sisters in a long time. She didn't want to lose it now.

Before Kristen found words to let Maddy know that she was okay, the bedroom door opened and Sam entered. His gaze went first to Maddy, a quick appraisal as if to reassure himself that she was still there and still okay.

When he shifted his gaze to Kristen, his eyes widened a little, no doubt with surprise at finding his daughter's bodyguard weeping like a baby. She looked down, mortified, wiping away the rest of the moisture clinging to her cheeks and eyelashes in a couple of brisk swipes.

Sam crossed to the bed. *"Horton Hears a Who,"* he read aloud. "Excellent choice, ladies."

As Maddy giggled up at her father, Kristen scrambled off the bed, waving for him to take her place. "Maddy was reading to me. We left poor Horton in a precarious place." She was pleased by the light tone of her voice. Maybe he'd buy that she'd been crying tears of laughter.

"But it's okay," Maddy insisted, her tone filled with childish urgency, apparently afraid Kristen was still worried about Horton and his tiny friends. Kristen felt an unexpected rush of affection for the little girl, touched by her concern.

"I'm sure Miss Kristen knows that," Sam assured Maddy, but Kristen heard a hint of puzzlement in his voice. She guessed he hadn't fallen for the "tears of laughter" attempt.

"Did your call go okay?" she asked.

He caught her meaning and gave a nod. "Let me finish reading this with Maddy and then we'll talk."

She settled against the door frame, watching Maddy cuddle close to Sam as he finished the story. By the time the jungle animals pledged to protect the imperiled Whovillians, Maddy's eyes had drooped closed. Sam bent and kissed her pink cheek, lingering a moment. Kristen had to look away, a dozen different emotions roiling through her. She'd never shared those kinds of moments with her father, who'd left the family when she was just six years old, and who'd been distant long before then.

Sam finally eased himself away from Maddy and joined her at the door. "Outside," he whispered, opening the door for her.

He guided her away from the door, stopping in the middle of the living room. "I don't want Maddy to overhear."

"Overhear what?" Kristen asked.

"That her mother's booked a flight to Alabama, arriving tomorrow," he answered grimly.

Chapter Five

"We're going to play a game, Maddy. Is that okay?"

Maddy looked up at Kristen, her expression curious. "But I'm coloring right now."

"I know. This is a coloring game." Kristen sat on the low stool beside Maddy's play table and pulled a blank piece of paper in front of her.

"A coloring game?" Instantly intrigued, Maddy scooted closer.

"I'm going to draw something, and you're going to help me color it in. Does that sound like fun?"

Maddy nodded, reaching for the crayons.

"I bet you have a good memory," Kristen continued, trying not to let Maddy's little girl smell distract her. She'd agreed to take this assignment to help Maddy remember more about the night of the attack. This might be one of the few moments she had alone with Maddy for a while, since her mother's impending arrival promised to be a major distraction over the next couple of days.

She took a black crayon and drew an oval. "I

know this might be a little scary, but I also know you're a brave girl. Aren't you a brave girl, Maddy?"

Maddy looked up at her, a hint of worry in her bright green eyes. "Yes, ma'am."

"I want you to think about the man who came to your house the other night. The one who scared you and made Cissy cry."

Maddy's eyes welled up with tears. "I wanna see Cissy."

The sight of Maddy's tears nearly derailed Kristen's plan, but she steeled herself against the little girl's emotions. The best way to help Maddy was to find the man who had tried to hurt her. "Cissy's with the doctor, who's taking the very best care of her. I know your daddy told you that."

Maddy nodded. "She's sick."

"That's right, but the doctor is going to help her get better. But right now, I need you to help me find the bad man so we can make sure he doesn't make anyone else sick. Okay?"

Maddy blinked away the tears and nodded.

Kristen pointed her crayon at the oval she'd drawn. "I want you to pretend this is the bad man's face. Can you pick a crayon color that matches the color of his face?"

Maddy picked through the nubby crayons and picked out a pale peach color. Caucasian, Kristen noted mentally. They'd been pretty sure that was so, but confirmation was good.

She took her black crayon and drew eyes inside the oval. "Can you tell me what color to make his eyes?"

Maddy's face crinkled with concentration. "No eyes."

"You mean you couldn't see his eyes?"

Maddy nodded.

"Was it because of his cap?"

Maddy nodded again.

Kristen drew a cap shape on top of the oval. "Can you tell me what color the cap was?"

Maddy's tongue slipped out between her lips as she studied the pile of crayons on the table in front of her. After a few moments, she picked up a dark blue crayon.

"Great, Maddy! That's very helpful. Can you color in the cap for me?"

Maddy pulled the paper in front of her and got to work, coloring in the blue cap. But she left part of the front of the cap blank, Kristen noticed.

"Why aren't you coloring that part?" she asked Maddy.

"It had ABCs on it." She beamed up at Kristen. "I know my ABCs. Wanna hear?" Maddy started singing the alphabet in an off-key warble.

Kristen steeled herself against a flood of memories. She'd taught the ABCs song to the littlest ones, Kevin and Julie, herself. By then, her mother hadn't cared much about her kids, except for sporadic bouts of manic mothering that left her younger siblings scared and confused.

"That's very good," she choked out when Maddy finished her song. "Do you think you know your ABCs well enough to tell me what letters were on the cap?"

Maddy's beaming smile faded. "Don't 'member."

"That's okay," Kristen assured her, squelching her own disappointment. Even if Maddy couldn't remember the letters, they now knew that the assailant had worn a dark blue cap with some sort of letters on the front. Possibly a sports team cap. It was, at least, corroborating evidence if they ever came up with an actual suspect.

"Miss Kristen, do you know my mommy?" Maddy's soft query caught Kristen flat-footed. It was the first question she'd asked about her mother since Sam left for the airport.

"I've told Maddy her mother's coming for a visit," Sam had told Kristen earlier that morning when she arrived to keep an eye on Maddy, "but I'm not sure she really understands what that means."

He'd told her that while Maddy had seen photos of her mother, and knew her name, she'd never spoken to Norah before, not even on the phone. Kristen wondered how Maddy was going to handle meeting a mother who was essentially a stranger to her.

Kristen pushed aside the drawing and turned to look at Maddy, who gazed up at her with worried eyes. Sam had dressed her in a pale green sundress and clean white sandals, and tamed her unruly brown curls into a ponytail at the back of her head. She looked adorable, even to Kristen's jaundiced eyes.

She wondered if Norah would be similarly impressed.

"No, Maddy, I don't know your mom," she answered the little girl's question.

Maddy slid down off her chair and crossed to Kristen's stool, tugging lightly at the edge of Kristen's denim jacket. "What if she doesn't like me?" she asked, her voice tiny.

Kristen felt a surge of sympathy for the child. "What's not to like? Look how pretty you look. And I saw your room this morning—it's nice and neat. And didn't you eat all your cereal and drink all your milk like your daddy asked you to?"

Maddy beamed at her. "And I took my vitamin, too."

"Well, see? There you go. You're a superstar."

Maddy patted Kristen's knee. "Are you afraid she won't like you?"

She grinned at the little girl. "No way. I ate all my breakfast this morning, too."

Maddy giggled and happily picked up the peach crayon, her curiosity apparently appeased. She reached for the drawing of the "bad man" and started coloring in his face.

Kristen watched her draw, trying not to let Maddy's last question nag her. It didn't matter to her whether or not Norah Cabot liked her, of course.

Which was good, because the questions she had to ask Maddy's mother wouldn't win the woman's friendship. Norah Cabot might have an alibi for the night in question, but that didn't mean she didn't hire someone to take Maddy from Sam's home.

And considering what she'd learned about Norah and her fiancé the night before, she had an idea why Maddy's mother might do such a thing.

She'd have a chance to challenge Norah soon enough. Sam was due back from the airport any time now.

"YOU'RE NERVOUS." Norah's voice was tinged with amusement.

"I'm wary," he corrected, putting the car in Park and shutting off the engine before he turned to look at her.

She looked impeccable, even after a plane ride from New York to Alabama. Her lightweight gray suit and cream silk blouse fit her perfectly, and her short, spiky hairstyle had probably cost a fortune. He wondered who she was trying to impress. Him? Or Maddy?

"I know it's been a few years, but I haven't suddenly developed a violent streak. I still don't bite." She opened the passenger door, unfolded her long legs and stepped from the car before he had a chance to circle the car and open the door for her.

He left her bags in the car, as he'd already decided before she arrived that she'd be staying in a nearby motel rather than with them at the guesthouse. "I'm surprised Graham didn't come with you," he said as he joined her on the flagstone walkway.

"So you've heard about my engagement." She flashed him a wry smile. "Graham had business back in Baltimore."

"I thought you were in the Hamptons."

"Only for a party. We were set to return home today anyway." She straightened her jacket and patted her hair as they reached the door, the first indication of nerves since he'd picked her up at the airport.

He opened the door and ushered her inside, then froze in his tracks at the sight in front of him.

Kristen was on the floor, on her hands and knees, apparently looking for something under the sofa while Maddy danced around her, shrieking with laughter.

Almost before he had a chance to blink, however, Kristen had risen to a crouch, one arm tucking Maddy behind her back while the other hand reached for the ankle holster hidden beneath the right leg of her jeans.

Sam held up his hands quickly. "We come in peace."

Kristen relaxed, dropping her hand from the hidden weapon and reaching back to swing Maddy in front of her. She pushed to her feet, straightening her blouse. A fierce pink blush washed over her neck and face. "We, um, lost a crayon."

Maddy's eyes lit up as she spotted him. "We've been drawing, Daddy!"

"So I see." Sam let his gaze slide from his daughter's bright face to Kristen Tandy's mortified expression. He smiled, amused and a little touched by her embarrassment at being caught with her pretty little butt in the air. She managed a sheepish smile in return, and his stomach did a flip.

Maddy caught sight of Norah standing in the doorway behind him, and her broad grin faded to a tentative half smile.

Sam crossed to his daughter's side and took her hand, leading her to where Norah stood. "Maddy, this is your mother, Norah. Norah, this is Maddy."

Norah took Maddy's hand. "It's nice to meet you, Maddy."

"You're pretty," Maddy blurted, and Sam smiled.

Norah chuckled. "Thank you. You're pretty, too." She released Maddy's hand and straightened, looking around the guesthouse with a speculative gaze. "So this is the famous Cooper Cove Marina and Fishing Camp."

"Technically, it's my parents' guesthouse," he corrected lightly, trying not to let the mild disdain in her tone annoy him. "Would you like some coffee? A glass of tea?"

"God, not that sweet treacle you Southerners call tea." She shed her suit jacket, baring a pair of slim, toned arms. She hadn't been letting herself go over the past four years, he saw. She was as trim and beautiful as ever.

He took the jacket from her and hung it on the

rack by the door. He turned back to find Norah looking quizzically at Kristen.

"Norah Cabot," she introduced herself, crossing to where Kristen stood beside the writing desk near the window.

Kristen shook Norah's hand. "Detective Kristen Tandy, Gossamer Ridge Police Department."

Norah's dark brows lifted. "Is this an ambush?"

Kristen's smile looked almost predatory, catching Sam by surprise. "Funny you'd jump to that conclusion, Ms. Cabot, instead of assuming I was here to protect your daughter."

Norah shot Sam a murderous look. "An hour in the car and you couldn't see fit to warn me I was walking into a trap?"

"Ms. Tandy is here to protect Maddy," he answered with a shrug, enjoying his ex-wife's discomfort a little more than he should. It was a novel experience to see Norah caught off balance. She was usually in full control of any situation, whether a heated court battle—or a marriage falling apart.

"And to ask a few questions," Kristen added firmly.

Holding back a smile, Sam decided this morning might turn out to be more enjoyable than he'd expected.

THOUGH SAM HAD SPENT MOST of the last eighteen hours fretting about how to prepare Maddy for her mother's arrival, in the end, his worries had been for nothing. Maddy didn't seem to find anything odd about meeting her mother for the first time at the age of four, and Norah didn't overplay the mommy card.

Maddy enjoyed looking at old photos Norah had brought with her, including several photos from their brief marriage. She'd even agreed with Norah that they shared the same green eyes and long fingers and toes. But she made no fuss when Norah handed her off to Sam's brother Jake and Jake's wife, Mariah, after a tour of the family property. While Jake and Mariah played tag with Maddy and Micah, Mariah's two-year-old, under the ancient oak towering over the backyard, Norah crossed the lawn to the bottom step of the deck stairs where Sam sat.

"She's lovely," Norah said with a smile, settling onto the step beside him. "You're a wonderful father. But I always knew you would be."

Sam looked across the yard at Maddy, who was laughing with glee as Jake swung her around and around. "Why did you come here, Norah?"

Norah's brow furrowed. "Our daughter was almost kidnapped. Shouldn't I be here?"

"She was hospitalized with strep throat when she was a year old. We were in the same city then, and you didn't even call to check on her."

"The police didn't leave an urgent message on my phone that time. Pretty young Detective Tandy was so insistent." Norah looked over at Kristen, who stood alone, watching Jake, Mariah and the children play. "She's very new at the job, isn't she?"

"Don't underestimate her," Sam warned. "She's tougher than she looks." Anyone who could survive what Kristen Tandy had gone through as a young teenager was made of stern stuff.

"Have you taken on a new project, Professor Higgins?" Norah shot him a pointed look. "Looking to turn Daisy Duke into a proper lady?"

Sam pressed his lips together, already growing annoyed by Norah's blithe sarcasm. He must have found her witty and entertaining once, or he'd never have fallen for her. Maybe in a different situation, when his daughter's safety wasn't on the line, he might have been amused by her sharp commentary.

But Kristen Tandy didn't deserve to be the target of Norah's verbal barbs. Especially now, when she was facing down her own demons for no other reason than to protect Maddy.

"No comment, Sam?" Norah slanted another look at Kristen.

"Not everything or everyone is fair game for your tongue, Norah." He caught Kristen's eye and gave a quick nod of his head to invite her over.

She crossed slowly to where they sat, her expression neutral. But he'd begun to understand that her eyes were the key to deciphering her moods. Right now, they were a murky blue-gray, cool as a winter sky.

She didn't like Norah. At all.

"I suppose, Detective Tandy, you have more

questions for me?" Norah spoke first, her way of taking control of the conversation.

"Mostly, I'm curious," Kristen answered coolly. "After so many years away from your daughter, why show up now? I told you in my message that I'd be willing to fly up to Washington to meet you if I needed to speak in person. It seems a bit…out of character for you to hop on a plane and fly right down."

For the first time since Norah arrived, she lost her veneer of indifference. "You don't know me, Detective. You're not qualified to judge what is in or out of character for me."

The hint of gray in Kristen's eyes darkened. Sam could swear he saw ice crystals forming in their depths. "You abandoned your daughter to your husband's sole custody when she was three months old. You haven't seen her in person since then. You don't call Maddy to talk to her, not even on her birthdays or holidays. I think I'm perfectly capable of judging your behavior to be that of a woman who has excised her daughter from her life with brutal efficiency."

Sam stared at Kristen. Though he'd just warned Norah not to underestimate her, even he hadn't expected her to stand her ground with such ferocity.

Where had this little tigress come from?

This Kristen Tandy was exciting. Maybe even a little dangerous. He liked her like this, maybe more than he should, given the searing heat building low in his gut.

"The decisions I made about Maddy were for her own good," Norah said, her voice low and a little unsteady.

Kristen's lips curved slightly. "We agree on that point completely."

Norah's face reddened, and Sam saw the warning signs of a very nasty backlash. He stepped between the two women, taking Kristen's elbow lightly. "Detective Tandy, I had a thought about the files we were going over last night. Can we discuss them privately for a moment?"

Kristen dragged her gaze away from Norah and looked up at him, blue fire flashing in her eyes in place of the earlier ice. She gave a brief nod and walked with him up the steps to the deck. "What is it?"

"I enjoy a good verbal jousting match as much as the next man, but do you think you should antagonize Norah like that?"

Her cheeks grew pink. "Are you questioning how I conduct an investigation?"

"You're not investigating anything here," Sam countered. "You're angry at Norah for being, well, Norah, and you're letting that interfere with your work. You know damned well you don't get answers from people by insulting them." His voice softened with admiration. "Even if you do it magnificently."

Kristen's brow furrowed, but she gave a brief nod. "You're right. But she's such a sarcastic, snobby b—"

He pressed his fingers to her lips to keep her from saying the word. "It's half her charm," he said.

Her eyes flickered up to meet his, and he felt her lips tremble under his fingers. He dropped his hand away, the skin of his fingertips tingling once more.

"You like that in a woman?" she asked curiously.

"I guess I used to," he admitted. "Or maybe I just mistook her sharp tongue for spirit and fire." He lowered his voice even more. "I like spirit and fire."

Kristen's eyes darkened but she didn't drop her gaze. The air around them seemed warmer than before, as if the sudden tension crackling between them had supercharged the atmosphere. They'd moved very close to each other, he realized with some surprise, so close that his breath stirred the golden tendrils of hair that had escaped Kristen's neat ponytail.

She had beautiful, flawless skin, a dewy peaches-and-cream complexion that most women would kill for. He knew, without giving in to the growing temptation to touch her, that her skin would be warm and soft beneath his fingers.

He wondered if he'd be able to resist that temptation if this case lingered on too much longer.

She gave a soft sigh, her breath warming his throat. Dropping her gaze, she stepped away, looking down at the wide redwood planks beneath their feet. "Be careful, Mr. Cooper," she murmured. "Right now, Maddy doesn't really understand who Norah is to her. But she's the right age to start wondering why her mother's not around like other mothers are."

He cleared his throat. "I know. Believe me, I'm trying to be very careful here. But if Norah really does want to have a bigger presence in Maddy's life—"

"Did you know her fiancé is running for the open Senate seat from Maryland?" Kristen asked quietly.

Sam blinked. "No."

"Apparently he just announced his candidacy. He's up against a big family values candidate named Halston Stevens. Makes me wonder a bit about Norah's motive for coming here." Kristen looked toward the yard. Sam followed her gaze and saw Norah sitting in a lawn chair, smiling at Maddy, who was showing her mother something she'd picked up in the yard.

Son of a bitch, he thought. "How do you know this?"

"The Internet. It's this awesome new information tool—you should totally check it out."

He shot her a look. "Funny. Why didn't you tell me this last night when you told me she was engaged?"

She turned back to look at him. "I didn't want to poison your mind with the thought until you'd had a chance to see her interact with Maddy."

He rubbed his jaw, wondering if knowing would have made any difference. He'd been watching Norah carefully since he first introduced her to her daughter, maybe hoping to see some spark between mother and daughter that they could build on for the future. But so far, Norah's interest in Maddy had seemed little more than curiosity.

"I needed to know as much about your ex-wife as I could before she got here," Kristen continued quietly. "So I stayed·up late and did some Web surfing. Her fiancé's election bid is big news in Maryland. Local blogs are all over the story."

"You're thorough, aren't you?" he asked. She really was turning out to be a smarter investigator than he'd anticipated.

The amused look in her blue eyes faded. "Someone's stalking a kid. Your kid. Damned right I'm thorough." Her cell phone rang, a muted *burr* against her side. She dug in her jacket and stepped away, answering in a soft but terse tone.

Sam looked back across the yard at Norah and Maddy, his gut twisting in a knot. Was Norah really so cynical and self-serving as to push her way back into the life of the child she'd abandoned, just to keep scandalmongers from harming Graham Stilson's Senate bid?

The fact that he could seriously entertain the question made him wonder why he'd ever fallen for her in the first place.

"Tell her no," Kristen said sharply behind him, drawing his attention away from Norah and Maddy. He turned to find her shoving her phone in her pocket, her face pinched and pale.

"Is everything okay?" he asked, taking a step toward her, his hand outstretched.

She stepped back from him, grabbing the deck railing as she stumbled a little. "Everything's fine."

But clearly it wasn't. Her knuckles were white where she gripped the wood railing, and her eyes looked huge and dark in her colorless face. Ignoring the "don't touch me" vibe radiating from her in waves, he closed the gap between them, laying his hand gently on her shoulder. "You don't look fine."

She shook her head, ducking away from his touch. "I need to go into the office for a little while. I still want to talk to Ms. Cabot alone—do you think you could get her to the station in a couple of hours?"

"I'll get her there," he promised, his mind racing with questions he knew she wouldn't answer if he asked them.

Kristen gave a brief nod and headed down the deck steps that led out to the gravel car park at the side of the house, where she'd left her Impala parked next to his Jeep. Sam squelched the urge to follow her, instinctively aware that the harder he pressed her to tell him what the call was about, the more she'd dig her heels in and push him away.

Besides, it wasn't his business, was it? Unless it had to do with Maddy, and she'd have told him if that was the case.

Still, he had trouble dragging his mind away from Kristen Tandy's pale, shocked expression as he descended the steps to the yard and scooped his daughter up in a fierce, laughing hug.

Norah arched one perfect eyebrow at him. "Where'd Nancy Drew hurry off to?"

Sam ignored the barb, kissing the top of Maddy's head. "Maddycakes, I think I smelled some fresh cookies in the kitchen. Jake, Mariah, y'all mind taking the kids up to see if the cookies are finished? I need to take Norah to the inn to get settled into her room." He shot his brother a meaningful look.

"Ooh, cookies!" Jake coaxed Maddy from Sam's arms and swung her onto his back, where she clung like a laughing baby monkey as he followed Mariah and Micah up the steps to the deck.

Norah looked up expectantly at Sam. "You wanted to be alone with me at the inn, Sam? I'm flattered. But I'm engaged now." She waggled her left hand, where an enormous diamond solitaire glittered on the third finger. "Remember?"

"I remember," he said with a grim smile, taking her arm in his hand and leading her toward his Jeep parked on the gravel drive. "And that's why we need to talk."

Chapter Six

Tillery Park sat on the outskirts of Gossamer Ridge, Alabama, less a conventional city park than a protected patch of wilderness on the side of the mountain that gave the town its name. A few picnic pavilions dotted the park, as well as an old schoolhouse that dated from the late 1800s.

Beyond the schoolhouse, the land ended abruptly in a bluff overlooking Gossamer Lake and the houses that dotted its shore. A series of long stone benches stretched across the edge, only a few feet from the drop-off. At night, it was a favorite spot of the town's teens, who considered moonlit walks spiced with the danger of walking the bluff's edge to be the height of romance.

It was one of Kristen Tandy's favorite places, too, though not for its romance. Ever since she'd been a young girl, Tillery Park had been her place of escape, first from her troubled home life, then later from the stares and whispers that followed her around town after the murders. Her notoriety never seemed to follow her here to the park, where she was just one of the handful of townsfolk who came here to enjoy the area's wild beauty. People left her alone to think in peace.

She hadn't expected to come to Tillery Park today, however. Neck-deep in the Maddy Cooper case, when she got out of bed that morning she'd planned to spend the day with Sam, Maddy and Maddy's long-lost mother. She should be there now, instead of sitting on the hard stone bench, staring across the treetops below at the sparkling blue jewel of Gossamer Lake.

But that was before Carl's phone call.

"The administrator at Darden left me a message," Carl had said, referring to the state's secure medical facility where her mother resided. "Your mother wants to see you."

Kristen rubbed the heels of her hands against her burning eyes. Why now? Why, after all these years of blessed silence, did her mother want to see her now?

Her cell phone hummed. Carl again. She sent the call to voice mail and put the phone in her pocket again.

"Do you think that's going to shut me up?" Carl Madison's gravelly voice behind her made her jump. Her foster father stood a couple of feet away, holding up his cell phone. He had shed his suit jacket to accommodate the mid-May heat and humidity, exposing the familiar Smith & Wesson

686 Plus revolver tucked into a shoulder holster. He'd never gone to a semiautomatic like most of the younger cops. She hoped crime in Chickasaw County never forced him to choose a different weapon.

"How did you find me?"

He tapped the side of his nose. "Sniffed you out like a good detective. I mean, it's not like this is your favorite place to run and hide or anything."

Sighing, she edged over on the stone bench to make room for him. "You always did have an annoying sort of radar."

He settled beside her, giving her a light nudge with his elbow. "I'm a cop, blue eyes. It's my job to know where all the delinquents are."

She managed a smile, though her stomach was twisting and roiling. "I just needed a break from day care duty," she said, although if she were honest, she'd have to admit that watching out for Maddy was turning out to have pros as well as cons.

"Who's minding the kid?"

"Her father, her mother and a passel of extended family." Kristen couldn't hold back a soft smile. "She has them all wrapped around her finger."

"She's a cutie."

"She's a sweet kid. Sam's doing a good job raising her."

"What did you think of the mother?"

Grateful for the distraction from her own problems, she gave Carl's question the thought it

deserved. "I think she's very happy with living a so-phisticated, high-profile, high-power life. I don't think she sees Maddy or Sam Cooper as part of that life long-term."

"What about short-term?"

She told him what she knew about Norah Cabot's engagement to the Senate candidate. "The timing is interesting."

"You think her overture to the kid is her way of neutralizing any bad press about having abandoned the girl?"

"You know me. I'm a cynic."

"If you were really a cynic, you wouldn't be so affected by the things that happen around you," Carl said gently.

"You always think the best of me, don't you?" She couldn't hide the affection in her voice. Sometimes she wondered why she even tried. Distancing herself from Carl, the closest thing to a real father she'd ever known, hadn't worked no matter how hard she tried. He always came back for more.

"I *expect* the best of you," he corrected gently. "I know what you're capable of."

She looked away, feeling shamed and defeated. "You tried so hard to give me a normal life, Carl. But it was just too late." She ran the pad of her fingers over the knotty scar on the back of her hand. "I'm not a normal person. I'm never going to be a normal person."

"You're too hard on yourself, kitten."

Carl's use of his favorite endearment for her brought stinging tears to her eyes. She blinked them back, refusing to go soft. Not now, when staying tough was more important than ever. "I'm just honest, Carl. Too much has happened to me, you know? I don't have anything left to offer anyone."

The sad look in his eyes hurt her, so she turned away, her gaze settling on the sparkling water of the lake. Cooper Cove Marina was on the park side of the lake, just out of sight beyond the curving point of land barely visible to the east. Sam Cooper and his daughter were probably still in the backyard with Norah, trying to get to know each other again after such a long absence. "I think Norah Cabot's trying to be a mother to Maddy," she said aloud, remembering the woman's tentative overtures to her daughter. "She's just not good at it."

"You don't think her heart's in it, do you?"

"I'm not sure I'm qualified to judge."

"Sure you are. You're a cop." Carl gave her another gentle nudge. "What does that cop's gut tell you?"

"That Norah Cabot likes Maddy more than she expected to, but she doesn't feel like Maddy's mother. She probably never will." Kristen toed the dirt in front of the stone bench. "Some things you can never change, even if you want to."

Carl was silent for a long moment. When he next spoke, it was in a low, serious tone. "I think you should go to Darden to see your mother."

"YOU WANTED TO TALK TO ME?" Norah settled into one of the armchairs in her room at the Sycamore Inn. Challenge burned in her green eyes as she waved at the seat across from her. "So talk."

Sam ignored the invitation to sit. "Your fiancé is in a tough Senate primary battle with Halston Stevens. I know Stevens well enough to know he and his handlers will be looking for any dirt they can find on Stilson."

"Graham is a puritan. There's nothing to find."

"What about his fiancée, the woman who abandoned her three-month-old child to pursue her career?"

Norah's eyes flickered at his hard words, but she shrugged. "It's not like I dropped her in a Dumpster somewhere."

This time, he was the one who flinched. "God, Norah."

"You think I came here to meet Maddy so that when someone asked, I could say, 'Oh, I was just down in Alabama last week, visiting my adorable little girl. See—this is her latest photo. Doesn't she look just like me?'" Norah leaned forward. "Does it really matter why I came? Does it change anything?"

"Did you engineer this excuse? Did you hire someone to threaten my daughter?"

"Our daughter."

"*My* daughter." Anger burned at the back of his throat. "Norah, I have never tried to keep Maddy from you. I've always said you could see her whenever you want. But so help me, if you had anything to do with what happened the other night—"

Norah's eyes grew shiny, and her lower lip trembled, catching him off guard. "God, Sam, I know I was a terrible wife and even more useless as a mother, but if you think I could do such a thing—" She stopped short, licking her lips. "I suppose you think that a woman who could turn her back on her child would be capable of anything."

"I just want to understand why you're here."

"Because I was curious, all right?" She looked down at her hands. "When the police called, and then you left a message right behind them, I realized my daughter could have died the other night, and I'd have to live with the fact that I'd never really known her. You know, a three-month-old didn't even seem like a real person, but a four-year-old— I just—I didn't want to have regrets."

Sam stared at her, not sure whether or not he could believe her. There had been a time when he'd thought he knew her better than anyone else in the world.

Clearly, he'd been fooling himself. He was beginning to think he'd never really understood her at all.

"I didn't do this, Sam. I swear that to you." Norah leaned toward him, placing her hand on his arm. Her fingers were cool and light. "But I've been thinking about it, and I may have an idea who did."

KRISTEN LOOKED UP AT Carl Madison, horrified. Had he really said she should go see her mother? "No, Carl."

"You've never faced her. Not in all these years." Though his expression was gentle, his gray eyes were hard, like pieces of flint. "I think it's time."

"I don't owe her anything."

"You owe it to yourself."

She shook her head, rising to her feet. "We're not going to talk about this, Carl. If that's why you came here—"

"I came here to see about you. Period." Carl rose and stood in front of her, reaching out one hand to tip her chin up, making her look at him. "I'm on your side, kitten. Always."

"I don't want to go see her."

"Okay." He let his hand drop to her shoulder and gave her a soft squeeze. "Let me take you to Brightwood for lunch."

She managed a real smile. "Helen would kill me if I let you step into that diner. Think of your cholesterol, man."

"She has you trained, I see." Carl slipped his arm around her shoulder and walked with her to where she'd parked her Impala. He opened the car door for her, lingering as she slipped behind the wheel. His expression grew serious. "Kristen, if you want out of this Maddy Cooper assignment, I'll arrange it. I shouldn't have pushed you into it."

She shook her head. "You were right, Carl. I need

to do this. I think I can get a lot accomplished from the inside."

"Good for you." He gave her shoulder another squeeze, then stepped back, closing the door. He gave a wave as she put the Impala in gear and backed out of the parking space.

Reaching the highway, she headed south toward the office, remembering Sam's promise to bring Norah to the station so she could question her alone. But before she was a mile down the road, her cell phone vibrated against her side. She checked the phone and found Sam Cooper's phone number displayed.

She flipped the phone open. "Tandy."

"Kristen, it's Sam Cooper. I'm at the Sycamore Inn in town with Norah. How soon can you get here?" The tension in his voice made her stomach hurt.

"I'm about five minutes away. What's up?"

"I was just talking to Norah about some of my old cases and I think we may have something."

He was talking to Norah about old cases? Had he forgotten she was still a suspect? Tamping down her annoyance, she asked, "What kind of something?"

"A damned good motive for someone to use Maddy to hurt me," Sam answered.

"HIS NAME IS ENRIQUE CALDERON," Sam told Kristen the minute she entered Norah's room, eager to get her input. "His son, Carlos, was here on a student visa six years ago when he raped and murdered a fellow student at Georgetown University. Two weeks ago, while serving twenty to life in a Maryland state prison, he was murdered by another inmate."

He told her about the case, how he'd prosecuted Carlos Calderon despite his father's multiple attempts to buy off judges and intimidate witnesses.

She listened carefully, her expression darkening. "And since you put Carlos in jail in the first place, you think Calderon wants revenge?"

"Absolutely."

Kristen glanced at Norah. "Were you around at the time of the trial?"

Norah nodded. "I heard about Carlos Calderon's death soon after it happened, but since Sam was down here by then, I thought he might not have heard about it."

"How lucky for him that you had," Kristen murmured. Sam didn't miss the skepticism in her voice.

Neither did Norah. "What are you suggesting?"

"It's a place to look that we didn't have before," Sam said firmly, drawing Kristen's attention back to him.

"You said Enrique Calderon lives in Sanselmo," Kristen pointed out, shooting another glance at Norah. "That's quite a long reach."

"He's a man with a very long reach," Sam countered. "Calderon is one of the most powerful criminals in a country with its share of powerful criminals. He's behind much of the corruption that kept Sanselmo poor and dangerous for decades. He's probably funding half the terror attacks El Cambio and other rebel groups are carrying out in Sanselmo right now."

Kristen's brow furrowed. "And he's taking time out of trying to destabilize a whole country to kidnap Maddy?"

"Do you have a better theory?" Norah asked coolly.

"Maddy said the assailant was Caucasian," Kristen added.

"Maddy wouldn't know the difference between white and Hispanic," Sam said.

Kristen looked a little annoyed, but she gave a brief nod. "Okay. I'll look into his current whereabouts."

"We've already got feelers out," Sam said. "Norah has friends in the State Department."

Kristen looked up at him. "We'll go through our own channels," she insisted. If she was bluffing, it didn't show. Maybe she really did have her own channels, although he found it hard to believe a small-town Alabama police department could possibly have better intel than Norah's friends at State.

"Were you the lead prosecutor?" Kristen asked.

"Yes," he answered.

"So he would be likely to remember you by name, I suppose."

"And with his son dying just a couple of weeks ago—"

"The timing is interesting," Kristen conceded.

"I'll go call this in, get the ball rolling." Tucking the folder under one arm, she pulled her phone from her pocket and walked across the room to make her call.

Sam watched her as she spoke into the phone, her voice too low for him to make out words. She looked tired, he thought, her face a little pale. Dark circles bruised the skin beneath her eyes, bringing to mind her earlier reaction to the phone call she'd received at his parents' house.

The memory pinged his curiosity. Who had been on the phone? What had she heard to knock her so off-kilter?

He hoped it hadn't been bad news. She'd had enough bad news in her life.

"Quite the poker face." Norah's voice was low and amused.

He drew his gaze away from Kristen to meet Norah's bright green eyes. "Detective Tandy's or mine?"

Norah smiled. "The sweet young detective, of course. You're an open book, my love." She nodded toward Kristen. "Her own channels? As if a little cop shop like hers could possibly know anything about an international crime lord."

"You think we don't have our own share of big-time crime in Alabama?" Sam murmured, not sure why he felt the urge to defend Kristen Tandy when he'd had his own doubts about the usefulness of her connections. "A Mexican drug cartel carried out a series of gang executions south of here not long ago. It's a global economy, even for the bad guys."

"That doesn't mean Elly Mae Clampett over there can make a phone call and find out where Enrique Calderon has been for the last five days," Norah scoffed. "She just doesn't want to look like an idiot in front of you. It's kind of sweet."

Sam pressed his lips together, irritated by Norah's constant stream of insults. "Kristen Tandy is not an idiot. She's got good instincts, and she's putting herself on the line more ways than you know to protect my daughter—our daughter. There are things you don't know about her—"

As soon as the words escaped his mouth, he knew he'd made a mistake. Norah's eyes lit up with wicked interest.

"What things?" she asked.

A knock on the front door saved him from having to answer. He opened the door to his brother Gabe, who was carrying Maddy on his back.

"Jake and Mariah had to take Micah to the doctor, so they left the rug rat in my care," Gabe said with a grin.

Norah smiled. "Hello, Gabe."

Gabe's smile went a little brittle. "Hello, Norah." He lowered Maddy to the floor.

"Uncle Gabe's gotta go fishing," Maddy announced as she reached up to Sam for a hug. Sam gave her a squeeze, shooting a quizzical look at his brother.

"I have a last-minute afternoon guide job," Gabe

said apologetically. "We were in town for ice cream when I got the page. I called Mom to see if she could keep her down at the bait shop, but Miss Priss caught sight of Detective Tandy as we were driving past and demanded to come here instead. I saw your Jeep and figured you must be here with your ex." He gave a nod in Norah's direction. "If it's a problem—"

"No, that's fine." Sam shifted Maddy to his hip. "It's about time I take her home for her nap anyway."

"No, don't wanna nap!" Maddy protested.

"If you don't take a nap now, you'll have to go to bed early tonight. And I have big plans for tonight, let me tell you." He made a face at his daughter, knowing she couldn't resist a tease like that.

Maddy cocked her head, her eyes bright with curiosity. "Like what?"

He lowered his voice. "It's a secret."

Maddy gave a long, frustrated growl. "I hate secrets!"

"You love secrets," he insisted.

She sighed deeply and gave him a look that made his heart curl into a helpless knot. "Okay, Daddy." She gave him a hug. He hugged her back, trying not to squeeze too tightly.

"I guess I'd better get going then," Gabe said, nodding politely to Norah, then to Kristen, who'd apparently finished her phone call. He headed out the door.

"Quite the charmer," Norah said drily.

"You'd be surprised." Sam looked at Kristen. "Detective Tandy? Were you able to put out any feelers to your contacts?"

Ignoring Norah's soft huff of skepticism, Kristen lifted her chin and met his gaze steadily. "Foley's brother is an FBI agent whose area of focus is the identification and interdiction of South American drug cartels trying to set up shop in the states. Foley's calling him to see if he can figure out Calderon's movements over the last four days."

Sam glanced at Norah for her reaction. Her expression was a mixture of disbelief and annoyance.

"Well, I'm going to get Maddy home for her nap. Detective Tandy, didn't you want to ask Norah some questions?"

"Oh, terrible time for that," Norah said firmly, grabbing her purse from the writing table. "I'm afraid I made an appointment with Limbaugh Motors just down the street to obtain a rental car while I'm here in town. Give me a call later and I'm sure we can arrange something." She handed the room key to Sam. "Do lock up for me, Sam. I'll pick up the key later this afternoon." She breezed past them on a trail of Chanel No 5.

"Son of a b—" Kristen sputtered.

"Small ears," Sam warned.

She looked up at him, her eyes ablaze. "I'm not through with that woman," she warned, pushing past him through the door Norah had left open on her way out. Sam watched her go, enjoying the view of her denim-clad backside a little more than he should.

The next couple of days might turn out to be a lot more complicated than he'd anticipated.

Chapter Seven

"How did a Sanselmo drug cartel get mixed up in this anyway?" Jason Foley asked Kristen later that afternoon when she dropped by the office to see if his brother had called back.

"Apparently Sam Cooper was involved in several high-profile cases in D.C., including the conviction of a drug lord's son." Kristen explained what she knew about the Carlos Calderon case. "Junior ticked off a fellow inmate and ended up dead a couple of weeks ago."

"And Cooper thinks Papa C. has decided nabbing the Cooper kid will exact some sort of vengeance?" Foley looked skeptical.

"It was Norah Cabot's idea, actually." Kristen tried not to let her dislike show. "But it's certainly a motive worth investigating," she added grudgingly.

"What did you think of the former Mrs. Cooper?" Foley asked in a tone suggesting he already knew the answer.

Kristen tried to be fair. "She's smart, beautiful and sophisticated, befitting a high-powered corporate attorney. Seems to harbor no ill will toward Cooper."

"How'd she interact with the kid?"

Kristen thought about how she'd phrased it earlier to Carl. "She's kind to Maddy, and seems to like her. But I just don't get any sense that they connect like you'd think a mother and child would."

"And your theory about the fiancé's Senate run?"

"I still think that probably explains why she hopped a plane and flew down here so fast, but I can't really see where it supplies a motive for trying to kidnap Maddy from her father's home. Sam Cooper is open to Norah seeing more of Maddy, so why break the law when she could accomplish the same thing through normal, legal means?"

"So we mark her off the list?"

With a sigh, Kristen nodded. "Probably."

Foley chuckled. "Don't sound so disappointed."

"I'm not." She had to smile. "Well, not much. But if that woman looks at me like I'm some inbred hick idiot one more time—"

The phone rang, keeping Foley from saying whatever he was clearly itching to say. His wry grin faded immediately. He listened to whoever was on the other line for over a minute, jotting notes on the pad in front of him. Finally, he put down his pen and looked up at Kristen. "Thanks, Rick. I'll tell her what you found."

Kristen's gut tightened as he hung up the phone. "Was that your brother? Does he know something about Enrique Calderon?"

Foley nodded. "He found out where Calderon was the night of the attack on Sam Cooper's niece and daughter."

"SAM COOPER, A GOURMET CHEF. Who'd have believed it?" Norah lifted the lid and sniffed the savory aroma rising from the stew pot. She'd arrived at the guesthouse a half hour earlier, driving a shiny red Mercedes convertible with a Limbaugh Motors sticker and dealer plates. Sam suspected Mike Limbaugh had rented Norah his personal car, since the small dealership wasn't known for its luxury vehicles.

"It's just chicken-vegetable soup," he said aloud, mildly amused by Norah's hyperbole. "You chop a few vegetables, add some chunk chicken, water and seasonings and let it all simmer together. You should try it. It'll knock Junior's socks off."

She made a face at him. "I'm just surprised you turned out to be such a good hausfrau. You were always a take-out menu sort of man back in the day."

"Perhaps because you were always a take-out menu sort of woman." Sam stirred the soup. "I'm working fewer hours these days, and I have a child to feed."

As he reached for the pepper mill, he heard footsteps on the stairs outside. Automatically he went tense, reaching for the knife lying on the chopping board nearby and wishing his Glock 9 mm wasn't hidden in a box at the top of his closet.

Norah looked up with alarm. "Sam?"

A knock on the door eased his tension only marginally. Keeping the knife in his right hand, he crossed to the door and looked out. It was Kristen Tandy. He relaxed, reaching for the door handle.

Behind him, Norah's cell phone rang. He heard her answer as he opened the door and greeted Kristen.

"I have news," she said tersely, not waiting to be invited inside.

Sam closed the door behind her and followed Kristen into the room. Norah joined them, her eyes bright.

In unison, both women blurted, "Enrique Calderon is dead."

The twinge of disappointment Sam felt upon hearing the news that one of their best leads had dried up gave way to amusement as Norah and Kristen stared at each other in disbelief.

"How the hell did you know that?" Norah asked Kristen. "My contact at State called me the second he found out."

Kristen smiled placidly. "My contact called a half hour ago with the news."

"When did he die?" Sam asked.

Both women turned to look at him as if suddenly

realizing they weren't alone in the room. Kristen answered first. "The last time anyone saw him alive was five days ago. The FBI's source within the cartel confirmed Calderon's been dead at least four of those days—he saw the leader's body himself. The cartel's inner sanctum has been keeping things mum while they jockey for position in the leadership stakes."

Sam glanced at Norah to see if she had anything else to add. She looked annoyed but didn't contradict anything Kristen had said.

"Well," he said, before the tension in the room blew up in his face, "I guess we can mark Calderon off the list, then."

Kristen nodded. "But I think your case history is probably a good place to keep looking," she added. "There are bound to be others like Calderon in your past."

"Does this mean you're taking me off the suspect list, Detective?" Norah asked drily.

Kristen turned to Norah, her gaze narrowed. "I can't see where you'd have any motive to try to harm Maddy or Sam. They've made it clear that you're welcome to have a part in their lives, so you'd have no reason to take extreme measures to be with your child."

"Well, hallelujah. The Gossamer Ridge Constabulary takes me off the most-wanted list." Norah feigned relief.

"Perhaps you'd prefer we skip steps and leave

stones unturned in our quest to protect your daughter," Kristen responded quietly.

Norah's expression went serious. "No. I would not prefer that, Detective."

"I think I hear Maddy stirring from her nap," Sam interjected. "We didn't discuss dinner, Detective Tandy, but there's plenty for everyone. Unless you have other plans?"

Norah spoke before Kristen could answer. "Actually, Sam, would you mind terribly if I took Maddy out for dinner tonight? The Sycamore Inn has a lovely little French café on the first floor. I thought Maddy and I could eat there and get a little better acquainted. Just the two of us."

Sam's gut twisted at the request, catching him by surprise. He had thought he would be happy to see Norah take an interest in their daughter, but the idea of handing Maddy over to the mother she barely knew suddenly held no appeal for him.

"I'm not sure it's safe, given what's been happening," Kristen interjected. Sam flashed her a grateful look.

"Oh, please. We won't be walking down Main Street flashing a 'come and get us' sign," Norah scoffed. "I just want a little alone time with my daughter at a perfectly safe little inn in downtown Gossamer Ridge." She put her hand on Sam's arm. "You always say I can see Maddy whenever I want, no conditions. I want to take her to dinner. Please trust me to do that."

Sam glanced at Kristen, wondering if she'd come up with another argument. "I don't think someone will go after her in a public place," Kristen said, her watchful gaze batting the ball back into his court.

With a sigh, he turned back to Norah. "Her bedtime is eight-thirty. I'll go see if she's up from her nap."

Sam moved reluctantly toward the bedroom door, half expecting a fight to break out the second his back was turned. But both Norah and Kristen remained silent as he opened the door and slipped into the darkened bedroom.

He crossed to the bed and turned on the small bedside lamp. Pale gold light illuminated his daughter's sleepy face. "Is it time for my surprise?" she asked, her voice hoarse from the nap.

Trust his little girl to have a sharp memory when it came to promised treats. The surprise he'd promised was the batch of peanut butter fudge his mom had made the night before and packed up for him earlier when they were at his parents' house, but now he had a different surprise. "How would you like to go to dinner with just your mommy tonight?"

"Mommy?" Maddy sounded a little doubtful, as if she had expected to wake to find Norah already gone.

Sam's heart spasmed. "Your mother wants to take you to the inn where she's staying to have dinner. Just the two of you. Wouldn't you like that? A girls' night out?"

Maddy's forehead wrinkled. "Just Mommy and me?"

Sam nodded. "It'll be fun. I bet she'll even buy you some chocolate ice cream for dessert." He made a mental note to make sure Norah did just that.

"Well, okay," Maddy said after a moment. "Can I wear my purple dress?"

He smiled, relieved he'd thought to pack it. "You betcha." He went to the closet and pulled down her favorite purple sundress, the one with the bright yellow sash and the enormous sunflower right in the middle. Maddy loved to wear it for special occasions like birthdays and parties. Maybe it was a good sign that she was excited enough about dinner with her mother to think of the purple dress.

As he helped her into the dress and brushed her hair, he found his mind wandering away from the idea of Norah and Maddy out on the town together and into the dangerous territory of dinner alone with Kristen Tandy. Would she agree to stay for dinner, without the buffer of Maddy between them? Did she even feel the same tension he felt every time they were alone together?

"Ready to go, baby?" he asked Maddy when he'd finished putting her hair up in a neat ponytail.

"Come with us, Daddy."

"I can't, sweetie. Your mama wants to take you to dinner all by herself. And besides, if I go, Miss Kristen will have to eat dinner all alone. You don't want that, do you?"

She looked inclined to argue, but he hurried her out to the living room, where he found Kristen and Norah standing about as far apart as they could manage.

Norah smiled at Maddy. "You look so pretty, Maddy," she proclaimed, although Sam could almost see her mind clicking off a list of ways she'd have dressed Maddy differently. He hoped she'd keep her constructive criticism to herself around Maddy.

He resisted the temptation to walk Maddy and Norah out to the car, appeasing himself by watching them drive away through the front window, his heart in his throat.

"I think she'll be fine with your ex-wife," Kristen said softly. Her voice was close; when he turned to face her, he found her standing only a foot or so away.

"I know. I'm being an idiot." He managed a smile. "You know, the dinner invitation stands. I have a big pot of chicken soup and nobody to share it with. Do you have dinner plans?"

She shot him a wry smile. "No plans."

He held out his arm. "Your table awaits, madam."

She cocked her head, surprise tinting her expression. But she slipped her hand into the crook of his arm and smiled up at him, letting him walk her over to the table.

She didn't sit immediately when he pulled out her chair. "Don't you need help in the kitchen?"

"Are you impugning my culinary skills?"

"No, of course not." She sat when he waved his hand insistently at the chair, but her voice followed him into the kitchen. "But I could at least get some ice in the glasses."

He turned to look at her, amused by her obvious unease at being waited on. "Let me do this for you. Consider it a thank-you for what you're doing for Maddy."

She looked as if she wanted to argue but finally gave a nod of assent and settled in the chair, her hands folded primly in her lap. She looked nervous—adorably so, like a teenager on her first formal date. Well, except for the teenager part. There was nothing girlish in the way her curvy body filled out her faded jeans and fitted gray blouse.

He spooned soup into two bowls and carried them to the table. "Today's chicken soup includes a dash of sea salt, a delicate sprinkle of chicken bouillon powder and a bold, ambitious canned vegetable blend."

She grinned up at him. "Don't you hate when waiters do that? Like it's going to make the entrée taste better if you know the mushrooms were grown in the basement of a tiny monastery in France."

He grinned back at her, pleased she got the joke. "Especially when you know they were probably grown accidentally in the leaky basement beneath the restaurant."

"Exactly!"

He returned to the kitchen for the iced tea, still smiling. Maybe this evening would turn out even better than he had hoped.

AN HOUR LATER, KRISTEN HAD finally let herself relax. Sam was a funny, entertaining dinner companion, seeming to instinctively steer clear of touchy subjects during the meal. Instead, he told her stories about his time in the JAG corps, with himself as the butt of most of the jokes. By the time they moved to the living room for the whipped cream and strawberry dessert, Kristen had begun to wonder why she'd felt so nervous about sticking around.

"My mother grows strawberries in a little garden beside the house," he told her, setting the bowl of fruit and cream in front of her. "She has an amazing green thumb. The garden is tiny—maybe twenty feet long by six feet wide, but she gets the most out of the soil. Strawberries, blueberries, turnip greens, green beans, tomatoes—one year she even grew corn."

"I always wanted a garden," Kristen admitted. "I tried once, when I was about ten. I wanted to grow flowers—daisies and irises and roses. Our neighbor down the street, Mrs. Tamberlain, had the most beautiful rose garden. One day she gave me a cutting and told me how to get it to root in water so I could plant it myself." She smiled at the memory. "When the roots started to sprout from the cuttings,

I was so excited I started jumping around like I'd won the lottery or something."

"Did it grow?"

Her smile faded. "Mama got angry at me about something—I don't even remember what now. She threw the glass holding the roses at the refrigerator. It smashed all over the place. And she just stomped over the roses to make me cry." She pressed her lips to a tight line, anger and hurt bubbling up from a place deep inside her, a place she thought she'd shut down a long time ago. "But I didn't cry."

She felt his gaze on her, knew what she'd see if she looked at him. Pity. Maybe horror. Probably both.

She cleared her throat and picked up the bowl of strawberries and cream, even though her appetite was long gone.

"You don't talk about your childhood much, I imagine," Sam said. He didn't sound pitying or horrified, just curious. She dared a quick look at him. He met her gaze almost impassively.

"No, I don't," she admitted.

"I should warn you, I talk about mine all the time. Growing up here by the lake was any kid's dream come true." He took a bite of dessert. "I know I'm lucky."

"You are." She took a bite of the strawberries and cream, as well. The flavor was the perfect blend of sweet and tart, and the appetite that had fled with her memories came roaring back with a vengeance. "These strawberries are amazing."

"Told you." He gave her a light nudge with his elbow. "Next time we're up at the main house, get Mom to show you her tomatoes. She might give you a cutting so you can grow some of your own."

"Nowhere to grow tomatoes at my apartment."

"Not even a sunny balcony or porch?"

She did have a small, sunny patio at the back of her apartment, facing the grassy courtyard of the apartment complex. "I guess I could grow them in large planters."

"That's the spirit. You'll be a gardener in no time." Sam set his empty bowl on the table in front of him. "Sometimes you don't get exactly what you want in life, you know. But if you're creative and maybe a little brave, you can usually get pretty damned close."

He wasn't just talking about gardens anymore, she knew. But he was talking as someone who'd had a pretty good life. Maybe his first marriage hadn't worked out, but he had the kind of family background that made it easy to pick himself up and move on to the next challenge.

She didn't have that kind of foundation. She didn't even know what a normal life looked like.

"You and Maddy seemed to be having fun when we got here." Sam reached across the coffee table and picked up the drawing Kristen and Maddy had been working on earlier. "I guess you're developing a little resistance to your kid allergy, huh?"

"I don't have a kid allergy," she replied. "They just—"

"Bring back bad memories?"

She looked up at him. "Yeah."

He nodded, his expression solemn but mercifully devoid of pity. "I figured it might be something like that."

She didn't want to talk about her childhood, but the emotions roiling inside her chest were clamoring to get out, and she was tired of fighting them. Sam Cooper would understand, she realized on an almost visceral level. He'd keep her secrets if she asked him to.

"I was all my brothers and sisters really had, in the end." She had to push the admission past her closed throat. "Mama wasn't herself at all by then. She—she didn't exist in the same reality as the rest of us."

"You were a teenager by then?"

"Thirteen. Barely." She'd felt much older by then, however. Ancient. "It was like juggling a million flaming clubs all at once, while wolves were snapping at your heels. Trying to keep everyone fed and clothed, trying to get them to school on time, trying to keep social services from finding out our situation, trying to keep the little ones from understanding how far gone Mama really was—" She ran her hands over her face, nausea flicking at the base of her throat. Maybe she should have let DHR—the Department of Human Resources, the state's social service agency—know what was going on in her household. She'd been terrified that they would separate her from the other children, but in hindsight, intervention would have been so much better than what had actually happened.

"You know what?" Interrupting her bleak thoughts, Sam reached across and took her hands in his. His palms were warm and slightly calloused, pleasantly rough against hers. "You don't have to talk about this tonight if you don't want to."

"You don't think I need to get it all out?" she asked wryly. "Won't I feel all better if I spill my guts about my tragic past?"

"Probably not." His grip on her hands tightened. "But if you want to tell me about your not-as-tragic life afterward, I'd love to hear about that."

She smiled at him, almost limp with grateful relief. "That would bore you to death."

He let go of her hands. She tamped down a sense of disappointment. "Have you heard anything new about your niece?" she asked after searching her mind for new topics. In her haste to hurry back here to tell Sam about Calderon, she'd forgotten to ask Foley for an update on Cissy Cooper's condition.

"I ran by the hospital to check on her before I picked Norah up at the airport. She's still in a coma, though the doctor says he's more optimistic she may not have lasting brain damage once she comes out of it."

"That's good news, isn't it?" Impulsively, Kristen squeezed his arm, her fingers digging gently into the hard muscle of his bicep.

His gaze dropped to her hand, then slowly lifted to meet hers. The air between them supercharged immediately, making her fingers tingle where she touched him. She felt a hot tug deep in her belly, drawing her closer.

This was why staying for dinner was dangerous.

She should pull her hand away. Pull away and put distance between them, before she did something stupid and irrevocable.

But she couldn't move.

His gaze slid down to her lips, and she parted them helplessly, a whisper of breath escaping her throat. She saw the vein in his neck throbbing wildly.

Her whole body vibrated as the trill of a cell phone ripped through the tense atmosphere.

Sam jerked away, reaching in his pocket for his phone. "Cooper." He listened a second, his eyes widening with alarm. "When? How?"

Kristen's stomach tightened as she saw terror fill his eyes. When he spoke again, his voice was strangled. "Stay right where you are. I'm on the way."

He was halfway to the door before Kristen could react. She jumped up to keep pace with him, her heart in her throat. "What is it?"

He paused for half a second at the door to look at her, his eyes dark with fear. "That was Norah. Maddy's missing."

Chapter Eight

Norah met them at the door of the Sycamore Café, fear and guilt battling in her expression. Inside the small ground floor restaurant, the scene was pure chaos, everyone from diners to staff abuzz with interest and concern. A couple of Gossamer Ridge police officers mingled among them, taking statements.

Sam took Norah's arm and led her to a quiet spot to one side of the room, trying to keep from panicking. He slanted a quick look at Kristen, just to assure himself that she was there with him. She gazed back at him, her eyes fathomless. He grounded himself in their depths and turned back to Norah. "Still no sign of her?"

Norah shook her head, her lips trembling. "Nobody saw her leave, but—" She raked her red-tipped fingers through her hair, spiking it in a dozen different directions. "I had to take the call, Sam. I have a case going to trial in a couple of weeks. I couldn't seem to get reception in the bathroom, and Maddy told me she was fine, so I went outside for

just a minute. I told her to stay there till I got back."
Her face crumpled. "It was only a few minutes. It
took longer than I thought, but I swear, Sam, it was
only a few minutes."

Sam looked at Kristen again, struggling hard
against a gathering storm of despair. Her expressive
eyes were dark with worry, but she seemed otherwise calm, far more focused than he felt at the
moment. She laid her hand on his arm, her fingers
warm and strong, and he felt some of his fear ease
away. He covered her hand with his, giving it a
grateful squeeze.

After a moment, Kristen slipped her hand from
Sam's grip and turned to face Norah. "What did you
and Maddy talk about before she went to the
restroom?"

The question caught Norah by surprise. "T-talk
about?"

"Could you have said something to Maddy that
would make her run away from you?" Kristen asked.

Sam experienced the first glimmer of hope he'd
felt since he'd answered Norah's call. "You think
she ran away?"

"Kids run and hide when they're afraid," Kristen
answered, looking at Sam. "Remember the closet?"

Norah cleared her throat, and he turned his attention back to her. "Why would she be afraid of me?
We just talked about her preschool, how she likes
living in Alabama and about—" Norah stopped
short, giving Sam a horrified look.

Sam's gut tightened. "What?"

"I told her maybe I'd take her back to Washington. I meant for a visit, of course, but—" Norah turned suddenly to Kristen, closing her long fingers over the other woman's arm. "Could she have thought I was going to take her away from Sam?"

"She might have misunderstood." Kristen turned to look at Sam. "Call her name, Sam."

His heart pounding like a piston, he called out, "Maddy? Are you in here?"

The patrons, staff and policemen alike turned to look at him, the hum of low conversation stopping, then ramping up to a steady buzz. Ignoring their stares, he moved through the tiny restaurant in search of any place a four-year-old might hide.

Kristen joined the search, taking the opposite side of the restaurant. "Maddy, it's Miss Kristen. Are you playing hide-and-seek?" The two Gossamer Ridge officers followed her lead, spreading out to cover the other areas of the café.

Sam grabbed the arm of a waiter. "Where are the bathrooms?"

The startled man pointed to an alcove off the kitchen. Sam headed that way and found himself in a narrow, dimly lit hallway. The men's and women's restrooms were to his left, clearly marked. To his right were two unmarked doors. He tried the first one. Locked.

The handle of the second door turned easily in his

hand. Inside, he found a small storage closet. Boxes and bins took up almost every inch of the space.

"Maddy?"

The small, muffled voice that answered him sent such a powerful shot of relief through his veins that his knees nearly buckled. "I'm not going with Mommy!"

"You don't have to, baby."

A small box near the back of the closet shifted, and Maddy's tear-streaked face stared back at him from the void. "Daddy's honor?"

He grinned. "Daddy's honor."

She squeezed out of the tight hiding spot and threw herself in his arms. He hugged her tightly, flattening his hand against her back until he could feel her heartbeat against his palm.

"Is she okay?" Kristen asked just behind him.

He eased his grip on Maddy and turned to look at her. Her eyes were soft with relief, and he reached for her instinctively. She didn't resist as he pulled her into his arms and buried his face in her hair.

She smelled good, like the woods after a rain, and where her cheek brushed his, her skin was as soft as a whisper. Relief faded into something darker and hotter, and he wondered if she could feel the sudden acceleration of his heartbeat as it hammered in his chest.

"Sam?" Norah's voice broke through the heated haze settling over his brain. He felt Kristen push gently against his grasp, and he let her go, turning toward the sound of his ex-wife's voice. Norah stood at the end of the narrow corridor, her expression tentative.

Maddy tightened her grip on Sam, burying her face in his neck. "No, Daddy!" she whispered.

Norah didn't miss their daughter's reaction. Her face crumpled, and she hurried out of sight.

"Ah, hell," he muttered.

Kristen laid her hand on his arm. "Take Maddy home. I'll make sure Norah's okay."

The offer surprised him. "You sure you want to do that?"

Her lips curved in a wry half smile. "I think I'm probably the most uniquely qualified person to do that. You know, being an expert on really bad mothers."

His gut twisted in a knot. Until he'd seen his own daughter's terrified reaction to Norah's unintentional gaffe, his understanding of what Kristen had gone through as a child was mostly academic. But if something as simple and harmless as a misunderstanding could reduce his normally happy-go-lucky child to a terrified, quivering mess, how much worse must it have been for Kristen Tandy, living day in and day out with a mother like hers? And to witness the murders of her sisters and brothers, barely escaping her own death at her mother's hand—how had she survived it?

No wonder she was so guarded with her emotions, so reticent about her inner life.

He walked with her into the main dining area, staying close enough to feel her warmth against his arm. The patrons and staff stared for a second before breaking into applause. Kristen's face went red with embarrassment as the restaurant manager came over to offer his congratulations—and dinner on the house.

Sam thanked him but declined. "I just want to get Maddy home to bed." As the manager returned to his post at the front, Sam leaned his head toward Kristen. "How am I supposed to get back to the lake? You drove."

"I'll get one of the officers to drop you off." She smiled at Maddy, who'd finally loosened her death grip on Sam's neck. "Maybe you can sweet-talk the nice officer into running the siren!"

"Don't give her any ideas," Sam warned with a smile.

Kristen grabbed one of the uniformed officers, murmured a few words to him and brought him over to where Sam and Maddy stood near the door. "This is Officer Simmons. He's going to drive you back to the lake."

As Sam started to follow Simmons out the door, Maddy tugged sharply at his collar. "Wait!" she insisted, and twisted her body in his grasp, holding her arms out toward Kristen.

Kristen stared at her a moment, her expression hard to read. Sam held his breath, wondering if she'd rebuff his daughter's offer of affection. He might better understand the difficulty she had relating to Maddy now, but he couldn't explain those nuances to a four-year-old. Maddy would feel rejected no matter what he told her.

Kristen's lips curved into a big smile and she opened her arms, wrapping Maddy in a quick but genuine hug. "Make your daddy read you *two* stories tonight," she murmured, her tone conspiratorial. Maddy grinned with delight.

Kristen's gaze slid up to meet Sam's. He could see the pain lurking there in their blue depths, and his heart broke a little for her, but for the first time, he also saw the spark of genuine affection for his daughter. "Thank you," he said, reaching out to touch her arm.

Her mouth tightened, and she turned away from him quickly. "Talk to you later," she tossed gruffly over her shoulder, and then she was gone, weaving her way through the crowd in search of Norah.

Sam watched her go, regret settling low in his gut. Tonight's events might have broken down a few of the walls Kristen Tandy built around herself, but there were still plenty left in place. It might take a whole lifetime to tear them all down.

Did he want to devote his life to such a task or drag Maddy along on that kind of roller-coaster ride? Wouldn't it be better to just step back and regain some distance from Kristen and her problems?

At this point, however, he wasn't sure stepping back was even possible. Maddy was crazy about Kristen, flaws and all. And despite his clear-eyed understanding of just how difficult a woman she might be to care about, he found himself becoming more and more entangled in her life.

It wasn't likely, at this point, that any of them would leave this case unscathed.

"GO AWAY, DETECTIVE." Norah Cabot's voice was muffled and weary behind the door to her room at the inn. "We can talk in the morning."

"I think we should talk now," Kristen said firmly, even though a part of her wanted nothing more than to go home and bury herself under the covers of her old four-poster bed.

"Are you enjoying this?" Norah asked faintly.

"No, I'm not," Kristen replied. "Believe it or not, I'm here to help you."

There was a brief pause, then a rattle of the latch. The door opened and Norah stood on the other side, clad in a red silk robe that nearly matched the color of her tear-swollen eyes. "Here to help me. I've heard that before."

"I brought tissues." Kristen held out the small travel-size tissue box she'd picked up at the gift shop downstairs before heading up to the guest rooms.

Norah released a huff of laughter and took the box from Kristen's outstretched hand. "You think of everything."

"May I come in?"

Norah seemed to consider the question for a

moment, then gave an indifferent shrug. "Why not? It's not like my night could get any worse."

"Believe me, it could," Kristen murmured.

Norah ignored her and crossed to a small credenza along one wall of the small but pretty room. "The inn was kind enough to send up a complimentary bottle of sparkling water. I would have preferred champagne, but I suppose this is one of those dry counties you Southerners are so fond of."

"If you want to get liquored up, I could drive you to the next county over."

"Couldn't you just direct me to the nearest moonshine still instead?" Norah tossed a couple of ice cubes in a glass with excessive vigor. She set the glass down with a clatter and drove her long fingers through her hair, tousling the already unruly curls. "I'm sorry. I can be a total bitch."

"But at least you're self-aware," Kristen said.

Norah slanted a look at her and gave a short laugh. "Yes, I suppose that's a plus." She held out the glass of sparkling water. "Can I interest you in a drink?"

Kristen shook her head. "I just came to make sure you're okay. Can I get anything for you?"

Norah's brow furrowed. "Why would you care?"

Kristen knew what she was asking. Norah hadn't exactly done anything to garner Kristen's sympathy since her arrival. But it didn't change the fact that she'd been through an emotionally wrenching couple of hours. "I just thought maybe you could use someone…neutral. To hear your side of things."

Norah arched one perfect eyebrow. "Neutral?"

"Well, more neutral than your ex-husband, anyway."

Norah shook her head. "Sam must think I'm a complete idiot. Not even thinking how what I said might have sounded to Maddy—so stupid."

"You didn't mean to frighten her."

"But I did." Norah's gaze met hers, fierce and angry. "I'm very good at my job, Detective. I have companies trying to hire me away from my firm every day. Senators and congressmen who want me on their staffs. When a question arises at the office, you know who they look to for answers? They look to me. And I'm always right." She laid the glass of sparkling water on the credenza. "But I haven't done a single thing right for my daughter since the day she was born."

"That's not true," Kristen said. "You gave full custody to Sam. That was the right thing to do."

Norah paused with her hand on the glass, turning to look at Kristen. "Come now, surely you think I'm heartless and cruel for abandoning my flesh and blood, don't you? That I'm selfish and thoughtless for not even checking to see how she's been doing all these years?" Norah sank against the edge of the credenza, her expression bleak. "Guilty as charged."

"You're just not cut out to be a mother," Kristen said. "Sam has told me that you made it clear to him from the beginning that you didn't want children. You didn't lie or pretend to be anything you're not."

"But I should have wanted to be a mother as soon as I saw my daughter!"

Kristen thought of her own mother and tamped down a shudder. "Wanting to be a mother isn't the same thing as being a good one. You knew the life you wanted wouldn't accommodate motherhood, and you'd never be good at it. Why drag your child into a life that would be miserable for both of you?"

Norah looked up at her, eyes narrowed. "I guess you of all people would know about bad mothers."

Kristen hid a flinch.

"I know what your mother did to you and your brothers and sisters," Norah added when Kristen didn't respond.

Kristen squelched the familiar rush of shame and anger, feeling even more certain of the decision she'd made earlier that day. She couldn't go visit her mother, as the woman had requested. No way was she ready yet. "Who told you? Sam?"

"Of course not. Sam's the soul of discretion." Norah's smile was almost apologetic. "See, I'm not the sort of woman who abides having my life pried into without returning the favor. As soon as Sam hinted that you were more complicated than you look, my curiosity wouldn't rest until I did some checking. So I asked around about you when I went to rent the car. Seems you're quite notorious around these parts."

Kristen looked down at the scar on her hand, re-sisting the urge to beat a fast retreat. After all this time, she should be used to people knowing all the ugly details of her tragic history.

"My mother should never have been a parent," Kristen admitted aloud. "So I do have some respect for your decision not to inflict yourself on Maddy."

"Thanks—I think," Norah answered wryly.

"You could do more harm than good by hanging around and mothering her if you're not cut out for it. Sam's a great father. He's done a wonderful job with Maddy by himself. If you know you'd end up disappointing them both if you tried to start playing Mommy now—"

The sparkle of tears in Norah's eyes caught Kristen by surprise. "I would. I hate that that's how things are, but I don't have it in me to change who I am at this point in my life."

"Then don't let your fiancé's aspirations push you into doing something that will hurt both Maddy and you."

Norah scraped her hair out of her eyes. "Graham doesn't want kids, either. But he knows it's hard for people to understand, and God knows Halston Stevens will hammer him about it. 'What kind of man would marry a woman who abandoned her beautiful little child? Do you want that kind of man for your Senator?'"

"The right thing to do isn't always the easy thing to do. Matter of fact, it's usually not."

"Thank you, Obi-Wan Kenobi."

Kristen smiled. "You gonna be okay?"

Norah nodded. "I guess I should call Graham and tell him what's happened." She walked with Kristen to the door. "I know I've been a pain since I arrived—"

"It's part of your charm," Kristen said, still smiling.

Norah returned the smile. "Like prickly and defensive is part of yours?"

Kristen nodded, realizing she'd finally made Norah recognize her as an equal. "Exactly."

Norah's expression grew serious as she opened the door. "Protect my daughter. Find out who's trying to use her to hurt Sam and make them pay. Will you do that for me?"

"Yes," Kristen answered. "I'll do everything I can to protect them both."

"Good." Norah managed a weak smile and lifted her hand in a goodbye salute. She closed the door, leaving Kristen alone in the narrow hallway.

When she reached her car, Kristen called the office to see if anyone was still in the detective's office. The Gossamer Ridge Police Department wasn't large enough or busy enough to field a twenty-four-hour detective's division, but there was usually a night detective on duty until 11:00 p.m.

In this case, she got Jason Foley on the phone. "What are you still doing there?" she asked. "Gina finally come to her senses and kick you out of the house?"

"Ha. She and the kids are visiting her folks in Huntsville for the night, so I thought I'd review some of the neighbor interviews from Mission Road, see if I missed any clues."

"Did you?"

"Of course not. I'm a seasoned law enforcement professional," he answered glibly. "Heard you had a scare tonight with the Cooper kid."

"Yeah, but it had a happy ending."

"Gee, Tandy, two days on babysitting duty and you've already lost the kid once," Foley said, clicking his tongue. "That's not gonna look good in your personnel file."

She made a face at the phone. "Need me to come in and help you go through the interviews?"

"Is your life really that pathetic? You're twenty-eight and single, Kristen. If you don't want to go back to kidsville at the moment, go pick up a guy at a bar or something."

"You're just full of good advice. I'm so lucky to have you as my partner." She made another face at the phone. "I'm heading back to Cooper's place. Call me if you need me."

"Wait a second." Foley's voice went serious, setting Kristen's nerves instantly on edge.

"Found something?"

"Maybe." He sounded a little hesitant. "New interview—Carl put a couple of uniforms on the beat to cover more of the area faster, and this one came in this afternoon. Interview with a neighbor about two doors down from the Cooper house—Regina Fonseca. Her daughter goes to preschool where

Maddy does. I know we're keeping the photos quiet for now, but the uniform thought to ask her if she'd noticed anyone paying special attention to Maddy."

"Did she?"

"Not Maddy per se. But apparently she got to talking about how hard it is these days to know who can be trusted and who can't. Said she'd freaked out when she saw a guy taking pictures of the preschool playground a couple of weeks ago—thought it might be a pedophile—until she recognized him as the photographer who does the class photos for the school."

"That doesn't automatically rule him out as a suspect," Kristen said, a little buzz of excitement building in her veins.

"No, it doesn't...."

"Good catch. I'll check it out in the morning." She rang off and started the car. The clock on the dashboard of the Impala read 10:15 p.m. She hoped Sam wouldn't be in bed yet. She wanted to get his take on what Foley had uncovered.

And, if she were honest, she just wanted to see him again before she settled down for the night in the guesthouse's spare bedroom. Her body still hummed from their earlier embrace, as if her skin had memorized the sensation and kept playing it over and over like a favorite record.

As crazy and dangerous an idea as it was, she wanted more, and her usual self-control seemed to have left town.

Parked outside the guesthouse, she cut the engine and sat in the dark, wrestling with her reckless desires. Beyond the ethical and procedural problems inherent in getting involved with a crime victim, she was as wrong for Sam Cooper—and his daughter—as Norah Cabot ever thought of being. She had bad mothering in her genes, for God's sake. Her mother hadn't always been a nutcase—what if having kids drove Kristen to the same deadly extremes? She couldn't really know, could she?

And yet—she'd been a good mother to her brothers and sisters when her own mother couldn't. The little ones had secretly called her Mommy, going to her when they skinned knees, wanted a cup of milk or needed a bedtime story read. Didn't that count for something?

Across the darkness in front of her flashed an image of her two youngest siblings, sprawled across the hardwood floor of their bedroom, covered in their own blood. Kristen squeezed her eyes shut, trying to force the image away, but the truth remained. She'd failed them in the end, no matter how good her intentions.

Was she going to fail Maddy Cooper, as well?

A knock on her car window made her jerk. She looked up wildly to find Sam Cooper standing outside the car, his face illuminated by the pale blue glow of a quarter moon overhead.

She rolled down the window, feeling foolish.

"Something wrong?" Sam asked, concern in his voice.

She pasted on a calm smile. "Just trying to talk myself out of this nice, comfortable car. It's been a long day."

"I set up the spare bedroom for you. There are fresh towels in the bathroom if you want a shower." Sam's hand settled on the car door, his knuckles brushing lightly against her upper arm. Awareness rippled through her, even though a layer of cotton separated her skin from his.

It had been such a bad idea to agree to stay here with Sam and his daughter, she thought. But it was too late to back out now.

It was too late for a lot of things.

Chapter Nine

Sam settled deeper into the welcoming cushions of the sofa, worrying through what Kristen had just told him. It didn't seem likely that the school photographer could be the man who'd been stalking his daughter. "Surely the school vetted him before letting him get anywhere near the kids," he said aloud.

"Probably," Kris agreed. "But people fall through the cracks of background checks all the time. And besides, the photos notwithstanding, since this guy is really targeting you, not Maddy, he's likely not a pedophile."

"So a background check wouldn't flag him as a risk."

"Probably not. I'm going to check with the school in the morning to get the photographer's name." She reached for the cup of decaf he'd poured for her, closing her fingers tightly around the mug. He saw her hands tremble.

"Are you cold?" He reached behind her to grab

the knitted throw from the back of the sofa. As he did so, his chest brushed against her shoulder, and he felt her whole body jerk as if she'd just touched a live wire. Coffee sloshed onto his leg, not quite hot enough to burn.

"I'm so sorry!" Kristen twisted away from him, setting the coffee mug onto a corkwood coaster on the coffee table. She pushed quickly to her feet, a look of mortification on her face as she gazed down at him.

"It's okay. These jeans have seen worse." He wasn't as sure about his mother's cream-colored sofa, although many more days of Maddy Jane Cooper and the sofa wouldn't have escaped unscathed anyway.

"I'll get a towel." She hurried out of the room toward the bathroom just off the kitchenette, returning with a fluffy green towel. "I'll pay for the sofa to be cleaned. If it can even be cleaned." Her brow furrowed. "I'll buy you a new sofa."

He laughed softly. "My mother will know how to clean it."

To his surprise, she looked as if she was on the verge of tears. "My mother used to get really angry at us when we spilled things. I'm usually so good at being neat and careful."

Something inside him seemed to break open, spilling sympathetic pain into his chest. "Kristen." He stood, taking a couple of steps toward her until they stood facing each other, only a few inches of space between them.

Her gaze lifted to meet his, and he saw a battle going on behind her dark blue eyes. But he couldn't tell what parts of her were at war, or which side was winning.

"I should go to bed now," she said, but she didn't make a move toward the spare room.

The tone of longing in her voice seemed to echo inside his own head, a match for the restlessness pacing the center of his chest like a hungry wolf. The overwhelming need to touch her eclipsed the myriad reasons why he should step away and let her go, and he reached up to slide a strand of golden hair away from her cheek.

She closed her eyes as his fingers brushed against her skin. Her lips parted, a soft, trembling breath escaping. When he trailed his thumb over the curve of her jaw to settle against her bottom lip, her eyes flickered open.

Fire burned there, out of control. It seemed to draw out the fierce flames coursing through his blood, until his whole body burned with hunger. He wrapped his hand around the back of her neck and drew her to him, covering her mouth with his.

Her response wasn't tentative or shy. She wound her arms around his waist, pressing her body hard against his. Her mouth moved wildly, matching his passion until his head spun from the sensation.

He ran his hands down her back, tracing the curves and planes, drawing a map of her body in his mind and memorizing the landmarks—the lean, hard muscles of her back, the dipping valley of her waist, the sweet swell of her buttocks.

This is crazy, he thought, but he couldn't bring himself to care, not when her breasts pressed against his chest and her hands moved restlessly over his rib cage, setting off fires everywhere she touched.

He tasted coffee on her tongue, dark and rich, with just a hint of sweetness. Lifting one hand to the back of her head, he held her in place so he could deepen the kiss, drinking in the taste and feel of her. She answered, kiss for kiss, sliding her hands up his chest, gathering bunches of his cotton T-shirt in her trembling fists.

She dragged her mouth away for a moment. "I can't—" She didn't finish before she rose to her toes and kissed him again, threading her fingers through his hair and drawing him closer.

"Daddy!" Maddy's voice, tinged with panic, broke through the heated haze overtaking his brain. He felt Kristen's body jerk against his, as if the sound of his daughter's voice had hit her like a bucket of cold water. She scurried away from him, nearly tripping over the coffee table. She caught herself and moved toward the door to the spare bedroom.

"Good night," she said, her voice strangled.

He didn't want to leave things like this between them, not with the stricken look of horror on her face. But Maddy called for him again, a rising tone of distress in her voice.

"Don't go to bed yet," he urged Kristen, and hurried to his daughter's room, switching on the overhead light.

Maddy sat upright in her bed, blinking at the sudden flood of brightness. He could tell she was only half-awake, gripped by whatever nightmare had dragged her out of her peaceful sleep.

He sat on the bed beside her, and she crawled into his lap, wrapping her little hands tightly around his neck. "Don' wanna go with Mommy," she whimpered.

"It's okay, baby. You're staying right here with me, you hear me?" He kissed her moist cheek, his heart twisting inside. He'd thought it would be good for her to have Norah in her life, but maybe they'd left it too late. So soon after the attack on Cissy, having her mother come to town had been just one more disruption in her life at the worst possible time.

She settled against him, already drifting back to sleep. When he felt her grip on his neck loosen and her breathing grow slow and even, he laid her back against her pillows. Standing, he tucked her blanket firmly around her and stepped back, looking down at his sleeping daughter with his heart trapped firmly in his throat.

The last few days had turned their lives upside down, but one thing hadn't changed: he would do anything in his power to protect his child, whether it was from a mystery assailant or her absent mother.

Or a mercurial, enigmatic police detective with

a troubled past, he added silently, the phantom touch of Kristen's mouth still lingering on his lips.

He closed the door quietly behind him and headed back to the living room, bracing himself to have a long, honest and almost certainly uncomfortable talk with Kristen Tandy.

But she was nowhere to be found.

STUPID, STUPID, STUPID.

Kristen stopped her car at the intersection with the main highway, pressing her hot forehead against the cool curve of the steering wheel, the last five minutes of her life running through her mind like a recurring nightmare.

How could she have let Sam Cooper kiss her? Hadn't she just been warning herself about the danger of entanglements with crime victims she was trying to help? It broke every rule of ethics in the book, and that wasn't even taking into consideration the extra-special problems that Sam Cooper and his motherless daughter posed.

No way in hell could Kristen ever let herself get involved with a man with a kid. She had figured out a long time ago that she was a bad risk for motherhood. Her genetics alone, with her crazy, homicidal mother and her deadbeat, absent father, would disqualify her from procreation. And what kind of mother could she be to someone else's kid when she hadn't even been able to stop one crazy woman from killing her brothers and sisters?

She should have protected them. She hadn't. The end.

She didn't deserve to have children of her own. And she sure as hell wasn't going to inflict herself and her nasty baggage on someone else's kid.

She rubbed her burning eyes and turned right on the highway, heading for the office. If she went to the office, she could at least pretend she was still doing her job, trying to protect Maddy Cooper instead of running away like a scared teenager who'd gone too far on her first date.

And wanted to go further still, a traitorous little voice whispered in the back of her head. Her body still felt hot and restless from her encounter with Sam.

Maybe Foley would still be around the office. She could help him go through the files again, see if there was anything else they'd missed. Work was the best distraction. It always had been.

She dialed his cell number. He answered on the second ring, his voice weary. "What are you doing calling at this hour, Tandy?"

"Just checking to see if you were still in the office."

"After midnight? I'm dedicated, but not that dedicated."

She looked at the dashboard clock. Almost half past twelve. She hadn't even thought to look. "I'm sorry. I lost track of time."

"Where are you?"

"In the car."

"I thought you were at Cooper's place tonight."

"I was there earlier. I just thought I'd head into the office for a bit, do a little catch-up." She grimaced, knowing the excuse sounded lame.

"After midnight?" Foley clearly agreed.

"Forget it. Sorry I called so late." She rang off and shoved her phone back in her jacket pocket, squirming with shame at her own cowardice.

She turned the car around and headed back to the lake.

The porch light was on when she arrived, but the door was locked already. Rather than knock and risk waking Maddy, she let herself in with the spare key Sam had given her.

Inside, all the lights were dimmed. Sam had apparently gone to bed already.

She locked the door behind her and walked quietly down the short hall to the spare bedroom. Flicking on the light, she looked around the room, noting that Sam had put away the bags she'd brought with her and turned down the bed. Fresh-cut daisies in water sat in a clear glass vase on the bedside table, a feminizing touch in the otherwise utilitarian room.

Kristen sat on the edge of the bed, fingering the delicate petals of the daisies, tears burning her eyes. Such a thoughtful gesture, the flowers. Sam had gone out of his way to make her feel welcome, even though her presence had to be a disruption in his already-upended life.

It made her wish she was a different kind of woman.

But she wasn't a different kind of woman. She was Kristen Tandy, with a homicidal mother and scars that ran deep, inside and out. That wasn't going to change, no matter how much she might wish otherwise.

"HIS NAME IS DARRYL MORRIS." Gossamer Ridge Day School director Jennifer Franks looked up at Kristen, curiosity bright in her green eyes. She shifted her gaze to Foley, who stood at Kristen's side. "Has Darryl done something wrong?"

Kristen darted a look at her partner, who sat beside her in a bright yellow chair in front of the desk in the director's office. Judging by the room's decor, the preschool bought into the idea that exposure to a plethora of bright primary colors was good for developing young minds.

They just gave Kristen a headache.

"We're hoping he might have seen something the other day when he was here taking photos," Foley told the director.

Jennifer's brow furrowed. "He was here taking photos recently? Are you certain?"

"One of the parents mentioned seeing Mr. Morris here a couple of weeks ago," Kristen said. "She thought the school had hired Mr. Morris to take photos of the grounds."

Jennifer shook her head. "We don't have any upcoming projects that would require his services.

Perhaps she saw someone else and just thought it was Mr. Morris."

"Someone else on the grounds during school hours, taking pictures?" Kristen asked skeptically. "With the children around?"

Jennifer's frown deepened. "No, certainly not."

Kristen exchanged glances with Foley. One of his dark eyebrows notched upward.

"Do you have Mr. Morris's contact information?" he asked.

The director reached into her desk drawer for a vinyl business card folio. She flipped pages and withdrew a plain white business card with the inscription, Darryl Morris, Photographer and a toll-free phone number.

Kris jotted the information into her notebook. "Thank you, Ms. Franks."

"Is he a danger to our students?" Jennifer Franks asked, her tone urgent.

Foley handed her his business card. "We have no reason to think so at this point. As you said, the witness may have been mistaken."

"We just want to talk to him," Kristen added. "Meanwhile, if you think of anything you've seen or heard in the last couple of weeks, anything that seemed out of the ordinary, please give Detective Foley or me a call at the number on that card."

She followed Foley out of the school office, side-stepping a boisterous kindergartner who'd broken free from the line of five-year-olds marching down the hall toward the playground. Foley reached out and snagged the little boy's shirt, tugging him gently to a halt.

"Slow down, cowboy," Foley chided mildly.

The boy turned and flashed a sheepish, gap-toothed grin at Foley before his teacher took him by the hand and led him back into line.

Foley was still smiling when they reached the car. "Gina's pregnant again," he said.

Kristen stopped short, looking at him over the roof of the Impala. "Congratulations."

He smiled at her. "Thanks. It was a surprise. We'd always figured we'd stop at two."

Kristen wasn't sure what to say. Foley's mood was usually easy to gauge, but his out-of-the-blue announcement had her feeling off balance.

Not that she didn't have a million reasons of her own to feel off balance, starting with her unfinished business with Sam Cooper.

He and Maddy had both been up and dressed by the time Kristen finished showering and dressing that morning. Sam's mother was there, as well, having brought breakfast muffins for everyone. She'd stayed until Kristen had to leave to meet Foley at the preschool, her happy, motherly presence providing a welcome buffer between Kristen and Sam. Sam had looked a bit frustrated, but Kristen couldn't feel anything but relief.

She wasn't ready to talk to Sam about what had happened between them the night before. Not yet.

Maybe not ever.

"Is something wrong?" Foley asked when she didn't make a move to open the car door.

She meant to shake her head and get in the car, hoping the subject would drop. So she was surprised to hear herself blurt, "How did you know you were good parent material?"

Foley stared at her, puzzlement written on every inch of his face. "What?"

Ignoring the nagging voice at the back of her mind ordering her to shut up and get in the car, she answered, "When you and Gina decided to have your first child, how did you know you'd be any good at it?"

Foley's bark of laughter caught her by surprise. "We were young and stupid. That kind of question never occurred to us." He nodded toward the car. "Get in and I'll tell you all about my first year as a father. We'll call it 'Nightmare on Main Street.'"

Kristen slid into the passenger seat and buckled in, kicking herself for bringing up the subject in the first place. She didn't mind hearing Foley's tales from the dark side of fatherhood, but she knew that her out-of-character curiosity was bound to stick in her partner's mind, long after he'd exhausted his store of anecdotes.

The last thing she needed was a fellow detective trying to ferret out the motives of her sudden interest in parenthood.

Her cell phone rang in the middle of a faintly horrifying story of Foley's first experience with projectile vomiting. She grabbed the phone quickly, grateful for the interruption—until she saw Sam Cooper's name on the display window.

She stared at the ringing phone, her heart in her throat.

Foley shot her an odd look. "You gonna answer that?"

She braced herself with a deep breath and answered. "Tandy."

"It's Sam. Anything on the school photographer?"

His voice was businesslike. Annoyingly normal. Comparing his calm tone to the nervous flutter in her stomach, Kristen grimaced. "We have a name. Darryl Morris."

"Darryl Morris?" The calm tone in Sam's voice disappeared. "I know Darryl Morris. And now that I think of it, he just might think he has a damned good reason to hurt me."

Chapter Ten

Excitement pushed aside any lingering unease Kristen felt. "Detective Foley's with me. I'm putting you on speaker." She pushed the button. "How do you know Darryl Morris?"

"About eight months ago, his teenage son was killed in a traffic accident. The other driver had been distracted by his kids, hadn't seen the light change to red, and he slammed into Charlie Morris's motorcycle. The kid didn't have a chance."

"What does that have to do with you?" Foley asked.

"It was one of my first cases when I joined the Jefferson County D.A.'s office. I was assigned to assess the case and see if any criminal charges should be filed."

"And you didn't file any charges," Kristen guessed, beginning to understand.

"Not criminal charges," Sam answered. "We worked out a plea deal—the other driver pleaded down to reckless endangerment, was put on probation and did several hours of community service as well as taking a remedial driving course."

Kristen thought that sounded fair, given the circumstances. But she wasn't the father of a dead kid. "Morris didn't think it was enough, right?"

"His only kid was dead. I don't think anything would have been enough." There was a hint of bleak understanding in Sam's voice, and Kristen knew he was thinking about Maddy.

"Did Darryl Morris ever threaten you? Send you any angry letters?" Foley asked.

"He was definitely upset when we told him about the plea deal. There might have been an angry letter or two—I'll have to check my files. But I don't remember ever feeling as if he were any kind of real threat to me."

"Can you meet us at your office?" Kristen asked. "I'd like to take a look at any letters Morris might have sent."

"I'll have to bring Maddy. I don't feel like letting her out of my sight today."

She glanced at Foley. "That's okay—Foley can use the extra babysitting practice."

Foley made a face at her. "I'd better track down Morris, make sure he's not making a Mexico trip or something."

"I could do that," Kristen said quickly.

"Actually, Detective Tandy, I need to see you about another matter anyway," Sam interjected.

Kristen ignored Foley's curious look, heat rising

up her neck. "I can be in Birmingham in about an hour," she said, knowing that further protest would only pique her partner's interest more.

"See you then." Sam rang off.

"Are you blushing?" Foley asked.

She frowned at him. "What?"

He looked ready to tease her further but stopped himself. "I'll drop you back at the station to pick up your car."

She spent most of the drive to Birmingham dreading her arrival, worrying over the "other matter" Sam wanted to talk to her about. Was he going to want to do an extensive postmortem of her behavior the night before? She already knew she'd thrown professionalism out the window. And his willing participation didn't change the fact that she was the one with the ethical constraints, not him. She was the cop. She was the one who should have behaved better.

The worst part was, she wasn't sure she regretted it enough. The memory kept creeping up on her when she least expected it, whether at a preshift meeting with Carl and Foley or listening to a pre-school principal give her a new lead on the case. Even now, with the air conditioner running full blast and the police radio squawking now and then, she felt Sam Cooper's warm lips moving with slow, devastating skill over hers as surely as if it had just happened.

She gripped the steering wheel tightly, trying to

drag her focus back to the case. She reached for the phone clipped to her waistband, thinking Foley might have had time to locate Darryl Morris by now. But before she even had a chance to flip it open, the phone rang, making her strained nerves jangle.

The number on the display was unfamiliar, an Alabama area code but not local. She flipped the phone open. "Tandy."

"Detective Tandy, this is Dr. Victor Sowell with Darden Secure Medical Facility. I'm the psychiatrist in charge of your mother's case."

"How did you get my number?" she asked bluntly. If Carl had given the facility her number, she was going to kill him.

"Your mother gave it to me."

Kristen felt the blood drain from her face. "How the hell did she get it?"

"I'm not certain. It's one reason I thought I should call you."

Kristen checked her mirrors and pulled over on the highway. She didn't want to have this conversation while navigating traffic. She put the car in Park and hit the blue light on the dash to flash. "Tell me what happened. From the beginning."

"I can't really discuss the details of your mother's treatment," Sowell answered. "I can only tell you that she's been allowed some privileges recently. Visitors now and then. We allow her to make phone calls on a limited basis, and we monitor them to make sure she's not harassing anyone."

"And is she?"

"Not that we've been able to ascertain. But she has had a visitor recently. A man showed up yesterday, introducing himself as a lawyer interested in offering her representation pro bono. He said he was with an organization that represents the mentally ill in criminal cases."

Kristen pulled out her notepad. "Did you get a name?"

"Bryant Thompson. But that's really why I called," Dr. Sowell said, his voice troubled. "We had someone check Thompson's credentials and that of his organization, Humane Justice, just to make sure he wasn't trying to pull some sort of scam. The organization exists, absolutely. There's even a Bryant Thompson who works as an attorney with the group."

"But?"

"But the guy who came to see your mother was definitely not the same Bryant Thompson."

"Daddy, when's Miss Kristen gonna get here?"

Sam looked up at the sound of his daughter's plaintive voice, realizing he'd been staring at the same page in the file for the last twenty minutes. Too easily, he'd let his mind wander from the case at hand to the memory of Kristen Tandy's warm, strong hands moving urgently over his body.

He cleared his throat. "Anytime now, baby." Kristen had called back thirty minutes ago to let him know she'd gotten held up and would be there as soon as she could.

She'd sounded odd. Troubled. Probably upset about the lines they'd crossed the night before. He supposed he should be, too, but he couldn't bring himself to worry about ethical lapses when every cell in his body wanted to give it another go.

He just hoped he'd have enough self-control to wait until Maddy wasn't watching.

He distracted himself by dialing the number of the ICU waiting room at the hospital where Cissy was being treated, asking to speak to someone with the Cooper family. His brother J.D. came to the phone.

"It's me," Sam said. "Just wanted to check on Cissy."

"She's moving around," J.D. said. He was trying to keep his voice calm—self-control was J. D. Cooper's defining characteristic—but he couldn't mask an undertone of excitement. "The doctor says it may be a sign she's coming out of the coma."

Sam felt a massive weight lift from his shoulders. "That's great news!"

"The doctor's not sure how much she'll remember, if anything, so I don't know if she'll be able to help you catch the guy who did it," J.D. warned.

"All that matters is getting her well." A knock

sounded on his office door, and Maddy jumped to her feet at the noise. "Go tell her that Maddy and I are rooting for her."

"Will do," J.D. said.

Apparently tired of waiting for Sam to get off the phone, Maddy went to the door and opened it, throwing herself at Kristen Tandy with a squeal of excitement. Kristen's wince, though quickly suppressed, made Sam's stomach knot.

"J.D., someone's at the door. I'll call you later." Sam rang off and hurried to the door to peel his daughter off Kristen's legs, swinging her up to his hip. "Sorry about that."

Kristen shook her head. "Just caught me by surprise."

"Miss Kristen, come see what I drawed!" Maddy held her hands out, her fingers wiggling with excitement, as if she could draw Kristen to her through sheer force of will.

Kristen pasted on a smile and caught one of Maddy's flailing hands. "Slow down, cupcake."

"Why don't you finish it up while Miss Kristen and I talk? Then when we're through, you can show it to both of us." Sam put Maddy down on the floor again.

Maddy looked ready to argue, but he gave her a gentle nudge toward the coffee table where she'd been filling a couple of his spare legal pads full of squiggly drawings. With a long-suffering sigh, she picked up one of the highlighter pens he'd given her to draw with and went back to work with renewed zeal, the tip of her tongue peeking through her cupid's bow lips.

"Sorry about the delay." Kristen settled into the armchair he indicated. He pulled up the chair's twin and turned it to face her, unwilling to have the bulk of his large oak desk between them.

"Everything okay?" he asked. She looked distracted.

"I'm not sure." She shook her head. "Doesn't matter. Nothing to do with this case. Did you find any letters from Darryl Morris?"

"A couple." He handed her the letters he'd culled from his files. "The first one is pretty straightforward. Morris asks me to reconsider the plea deal. His tone is urgent but not particularly hostile."

"I see that." She set that letter aside and picked up the second one. "This one's not quite as…diplomatic."

"No." In the second letter, Morris had informed Sam in angry language that he'd contacted the mayor to lodge a formal complaint against Sam and the district attorney's office for their decision to make the plea bargain. He also informed Sam that if the D.A.'s office didn't reverse the decision, he'd contact the media, as well.

"Did he contact the media?" Kristen asked.

"Probably. But Charlie Morris was a seventeen-year-old kid who'd already been pulled over twice for speeding and who had just dropped out of high school because he 'didn't like all that school stuff.' The driver of the other vehicle was a devoted father and husband who ran a popular pizza restaurant and volunteered at a homeless mission. Honestly, the media wouldn't have touched the story with a ten-foot pole."

"And he never wrote you again?"

"There's nothing else from him in the files."

Kristen's brow furrowed. "I guess we at least bring Morris in to tell us why he was taking photos of the kids at the preschool. Maybe if we keep him talking long enough, we'll find out if he still holds a grudge against you." She held up the letters. "Can you make me copies of these?"

"Those are the copies. I thought you might want them." He gave her the file to hold the letters. "Any chance I could take a look at the interrogation video when you're done?"

She shot him a wry look. "I think you overestimate the technological savvy of the Gossamer Ridge Police Department."

"You do record audio, at least?"

"We do. I'll ask Carl if it's okay to let you take a listen." Kristen stood up, tucking the folder under her arm. Sam was about to remind her of Maddy's request when she turned to Maddy on her own and said, "Now, Miss Maddy, you had something to show me?"

Maddy beamed at Kristen as she crouched beside her at the low coffee table. "It's me and Uncle Gabe, see? He taked me fishing. I catched a big catfish, see?"

"I see," Kristen said, sounding impressed. "Did your daddy clean it and cook it for you?"

Maddy looked up at Kristen in horror. "Cook it?"

"We haven't told her where fish sticks come from yet," Sam said quietly.

Kristen gave him a "now you tell me" look and turned back to Maddy. "I'm sorry, did you say catfish? Of course you don't cook catfish! So, that's you in the green dress, right?"

Maddy nodded, pointing her stubby little finger at some more squiggles on the page. "That's Uncle Gabe, and that's Rowdy—"

"J.D.'s dog," Sam supplied. "Mom and Dad are keeping him, along with Mike, at the lake while J.D.'s up here at the hospital with Cissy."

"And that's Uncle Jake in his boat," Maddy continued, pointing at a speck just above the patch of blue that Sam supposed was the lake, "and that's you and daddy." She beamed up at Kristen.

Kristen turned and gave Sam an odd look. Bending closer, he saw why. The stick figures Maddy had identified as Kristen and him were standing on the pier, holding hands.

"That's a beautiful picture, baby," Sam said. "Why don't you draw us another one?"

Maddy grinned up at him and went to work on a fresh page of the legal pad.

Kristen pushed to her feet and turned to Sam, keeping her distance, "no touching" written all over her body language. "I'm going back to the station to pass all this by Carl and get the go-ahead to bring Darryl Morris in for questioning. I'll see you later, Maddy, okay?"

Maddy looked up at her, frowning. "Don't you wanna see my picture?"

"You can show it to me later at the house. Make it pretty!"

"Okay!" Maddy turned back to her drawing.

Sam hurried after Kristen, catching up at the door. He laid his hand on her arm to stop her from leaving. "We need to talk."

Her chin went up, but her eyes didn't quite meet his. "I'll call to let you know how the interview goes."

"That's not what I meant and you know it."

Her jaw squared a bit more and this time she met his gaze, her eyes defiant. "You're not going to go all squishy on me about a stupid kiss, are you? Because if I'd known you were going to be such a girl about it—"

"You're projecting, Detective." He leaned closer, smiling a little as her lips trembled in response. "You don't want to admit how much it got to you, do you? So you pretend I'm just imagining that pulse in your throat fluttering like a butterfly."

Her throat bobbed and her eyelashes dipped to shield her eyes from his gaze. "Whatever last night was, it's not going to happen again. We're clear about that, right?"

His smile widening, he opened the door for her. "Let me know how the interview with Morris goes."

Not looking at him, she slipped out the door and disappeared down the hall.

Sam's smile faded as he walked slowly back to his daughter's side. It might have been fun seeing just how far he could get under Kristen Tandy's prickly skin, but she had a point. Sure, when the case was over and done, there'd be no ethical reason why he and Kristen couldn't see where their attraction would take them. But there were other reasons not to entangle himself with her, beyond the ethical questions.

Kristen was kind to Maddy, and Sam had no doubt that she'd give her own life to protect his daughter, but that didn't mean she was good for Maddy in the long run, did it? Kristen had been up front about her issues with children, even more than Norah had. Her reasons might be understandable, but they didn't change the fact that she didn't want to be a mother. And Sam couldn't pretend it didn't matter. He wasn't some young stud Marine ready for action with any woman willing. He had Maddy to consider.

Maddy already had a mother who didn't want to be saddled with children in her life. She needed stability, not more of the same.

He checked his watch. Almost lunchtime. He'd promised Norah he'd bring Maddy by the inn for lunch to try to repair some of the damage done the night before.

"Maddy, remember when I told you we were going to go have lunch with Mommy today?"

Maddy's little brow furrowed. "Do we hafta?"

He nodded. "We hafta. Remember, we talked about how Mommy didn't mean to scare you. She's not taking you anywhere without me, right?"

"Right," Maddy said, although she didn't look entirely convinced. "Can Miss Kristen come, too?"

"Miss Kristen has to work."

"Can't we go see Miss Kristen work?"

"Not today," Sam said firmly, though in the center of his chest he felt a flicker of unease. He already saw all the signs of a Maddy-sized fixation. He wondered how much worse it would get over the next few days, with Kristen living with them at the guesthouse.

A soft knock on the door pulled him out of his musings. Had Kristen come back? When he found a clerk standing outside, holding a manila envelope, he felt a twinge of disappointment.

"A courier dropped this off at the front desk a few minutes ago, sir."

Thanking her, he carried the envelope to his desk, relaxing a little at seeing a return address on the front of the envelope for a law firm he'd crossed swords with before. He opened it to see what it was about.

But inside, he didn't find a letter, legal brief or anything else he might have expected.

Instead, he found a stack of color photo prints. The top image was a close-up of Maddy and her mother, sitting at a table for two in the small dining room at the Sycamore Inn.

His heart in his throat, Sam fished in his pocket for a handkerchief. He used the cloth to handle the photos, flipping through the small stack of images, alarm swiftly giving way to a fierce and growing rage until he reached the last photo in the stack, a picture of Maddy cradled in Sam's arms after he'd found her in the storage closet.

Arrogant son of a bitch had been right there in the restaurant the whole time.

He turned the photo over, knowing even as he did so that he'd find nothing. The wily bastard wouldn't have sent the photos if he'd thought he could be incriminated by them.

But Sam was wrong. There *was* something on the back of the last photo—a message scrawled in firm, black felt-tip pen that made his heart freeze solid in his chest.

Your child for mine.

Chapter Eleven

Kristen's phone rang as she was belting herself behind the wheel of the Impala. "Tandy."

"Where are you?" It was Sam. He sounded tense.

"What's wrong?"

"Are you still in the courthouse complex area?"

"I just got in the car. What's going on?"

"Did you see anyone as you left the building wearing a tan windbreaker jacket and a blue baseball cap?"

"No, I didn't see anyone like that. Now tell me what the hell is going on."

"I got another packet of photos. It was just delivered. The staffer who took it described the person who left the package as a man in his mid-forties, brown hair, wearing a blue baseball cap and a tan windbreaker." Sam's voice tightened further. "The son of a bitch made a threat."

"I'll be right up."

"Meet me at the reception area. I'm trying to get

a look at whatever surveillance video might be available."

Kristen retraced her steps back to the District Attorney's office, where she found Sam in the lobby, holding Maddy tightly on his hip while he conferred with a couple of Jefferson County Sheriff's Deputies.

"Any luck on the video?" she asked.

Sam introduced her to Griggs and Baker, the two deputies who were apparently part of the office's security detail. "Baker printed a screen grab." He handed her the grainy photo of a man in a light-colored jacket and dark cap with a blurry cursive *A* on the front. "We think it's a Braves cap."

Kristen stared at the photo, remembering with growing excitement the picture she had helped Maddy color the day before. Maddy had chosen a dark blue crayon and said there was an "ABC" on the front of the cap.

"Could this be Darryl Morris?" Kristen asked Sam.

"Maybe. The photo's not great so it's hard to be sure."

Kristen's cell phone rang. It was Foley. "Excuse me a second." She stepped a few feet away and answered. "Tandy."

"It's me. I've got a bead on Darryl Morris."

"You mean you're looking at him right now?"

"Yeah—had to drive all the way to Birmingham to do it, too," Foley answered.

"Where are you now?"

"Parked outside the shipping company where he

works. He just walked in. Did you get a look at the letters he sent Cooper? Do we have probable cause to pick him up?"

"What was he wearing?"

Foley was silent a second. "Why do you ask?"

"Just tell me what he was wearing."

"Jeans, a tan jacket, blue Braves cap—"

Kristen looked over at Sam and Maddy, anticipation surging into her veins. "Oh, yeah," she said with a broad grin. "We have probable cause."

"DETECTIVE TANDY REALLY thinks he's the one?" Norah asked Sam later when he met her for lunch in town. She glanced at Maddy, who clung to Sam like a little leech.

Sam coaxed Maddy into one of the chairs lining the sandwich shop window. "He fits the description of the man who left the photos at the office earlier today. The police were already looking at him because of the angry letters he sent me after his son's case was settled. We think he's the one."

Norah took the seat across from him, careful not to encroach on Maddy's space. "Then maybe this is really over."

"It won't really be over until Cissy wakes up and is okay," Sam said soberly, thinking about the way his niece had looked the last time he'd visited her hospital room.

"Of course," Norah said with a sympathetic nod. "But Maddy is safe, at least."

He hoped so. After the scares of the past couple of days, he wasn't quite ready to let her out of his sight.

"I have to go back to D.C. I'd only taken a couple of days off to go to the Hamptons, and I've had a case blow up on me that I really need to attend to." Norah waited for the waitress to bring water to the table before she continued. "I've already arranged for the nice people at Limbaugh Motors to take me to the airport this afternoon. You don't need to worry about it."

"That wasn't necessary—"

"I think it was," Norah said gently. "I made a decision four years ago because I thought it was the right thing for everyone involved. I still think it was."

He looked down at Maddy, who was playing with the colorful place mat on the table, oblivious to their conversation. At least he hoped she was. "So, back to how things were before?"

"Yes." She leaned a little closer, her eyes full of regret but also determination. "I'll never be what she needs. We both know that. It makes no sense for me to disrupt her life every once in a while just because of biology. She won't understand why I always leave again. She'll think it's something she's done when it really has nothing to do with her at all."

Sam would never understand how Norah could walk away from her daughter, but he also believed she was sincere in saying she didn't want to cause Maddy harm.

It was time to let Norah go completely and move on. No more hopes for something changing.

Norah wasn't going to change.

"I would like frequent updates, however," Norah added. "To know how the two of you are getting along."

"I'll e-mail you."

The waitress approached with menus. Sam took one and bent to show Maddy what the children's menu included. As she weighed the merits of a peanut butter and jelly sandwich versus chicken fingers, Sam glanced at Norah and found her smiling.

"I was right," she said. "You were meant to be a father."

On that, he thought, they could agree.

"Are you going to sit in on the interrogation?" Norah asked later, after the waitress had brought their orders.

"Detective Tandy wouldn't let me."

Norah smiled. "She's quite the little authoritarian."

"She's right. It would be a conflict of interests."

"But she'll whisper the details in your ear later, no doubt."

Sam tried not to react to Norah's sly tone. She was clearly fishing for information about his relationship with Kristen, and since he didn't know how to define it himself, playing Norah's game would be folly.

"If she's as good at interrogating suspects as she is at interrogating innocent people like me, Mr. Morris should break in no time." Norah settled back in her chair with a wry smile.

Sam hoped she was right. Because if Darryl Morris wasn't the person who'd tried to kidnap Maddy, then Sam and the cops were back to square one.

"THIS IS YOU IN THE surveillance video, isn't it?" Kristen reached into the manila envelope lying on the table, pulled out the screen grab the deputy had supplied and slid it toward Darryl Morris.

Morris looked down at the photo, his complexion shiny with sweat. Morris had grown increasingly unnerved since the Birmingham Police had transferred him over to her custody. The interview room she'd placed him in wasn't air-conditioned, by design, but it wasn't hot enough to warrant the perspiration dripping down the man's sallow cheeks. He looked queasy, well aware he'd been caught redhanded.

"That could be anyone."

"Anyone wearing a tan windbreaker and a Braves cap."

"Exactly." Morris looked at Foley, who'd remained quiet to this point. "There's gotta be a lot of guys out there with Braves caps."

"Who also happened to send angry letters to Sam Cooper?" Foley asked reasonably.

"And took pictures at Maddy's preschool while Maddy was in attendance?" Kristen added.

"I'm a part-time photographer. Big deal."

"Apparently a courier, as well." Kristen tapped the photo.

"Jeez, okay. I dropped off a package at the D.A.'s office. Is that some sort of crime?"

"A terroristic threat comes to mind," Kristen said to Foley. "Wouldn't you agree?"

"I'd think that's fair."

Morris's eyes widened. "Wait a second—terroristic threat? Sure, I wrote the jerk a couple of letters, but I didn't make any threats."

Kristen pulled a piece of paper from the envelope and placed it on the table in front of Morris. It was a full-size photocopy of the handwritten threat on the back of the last photo.

"What does that say, Mr. Morris?" she asked.

He stared at the words. "I didn't write that."

"That was in the envelope you delivered to Sam Cooper."

"I didn't know what was in the envelope."

"Why not?" Kristen prodded.

"Some guy paid me ten bucks to deliver it."

"You needed ten bucks that bad?" Kristen asked, skeptical. "Come on, Darryl. You don't really expect me to buy this."

"'Your child for mine.'" Foley read the phrase

written on the paper aloud, letting his tongue linger over each word. "You lost your son in a terrible accident."

"He was murdered."

"Sam Cooper didn't see it that way," Foley said.

"Wasn't his kid!"

"But Maddy Cooper is." Kristen leaned closer, dropping her voice a level. "Must be hard for you, watching Maddy Cooper running around the playground, so full of life and promise."

"No," Morris said, shaking his head. "I think her father's a bootlicking political hack, but I'd never hurt a kid."

"How about a teenager?" Foley nodded at Kristen.

She pulled out another photo and laid it on the table in front of Morris. It was a photo taken at the crime scene of Sam Cooper's niece Cissy lying unconscious and still, her face wet with blood from her head wound.

Morris recoiled. "You think I did that?"

"Where were you this past Tuesday night?" Kristen asked.

Morris looked at her suspiciously. "At home."

"Anybody there with you?"

He looked down at his hands. "No."

"Nobody saw you at home?"

"I live up in Pell City, near the river. Not a lot of neighbors around."

"You took these photos of Maddy, didn't you?" Kristen pulled out the photocopies of the pictures

Sam had received, both the more recent batch and the set from two days earlier.

He looked down at the photos again. She saw his eyelids flicker, and she knew she had him.

"Why did you take the photos and send them to Sam Cooper? Why did you tell him, 'your child for mine'?" Kristen pulled up the chair across from Morris, settling down to look him in the eyes. "He denied you the justice you needed, and yet there he was, with his perfect, happy little child. It wasn't fair, was it? That he could go home to his kid while the best you can do is go see a headstone."

Morris's eyes welled up with tears. "Charlie didn't deserve to die. Yeah, he had some trouble, but he didn't deserve to die!" He wiped his nose with the back of his sleeve. "Sam Cooper didn't think his life was worth crap, or he'd have tried that stupid son of a bitch who ran Charlie over!"

"You wanted to give Sam a taste of his own medicine." Kristen kept her voice low and soothing. "Because he should know how it feels to lose his kid."

Morris froze. "No, I didn't say that—"

"Why did you take the photos, Darryl?"

"The guy paid me to."

"What guy?"

"The guy who gave me the envelope. He was right outside the courthouse—didn't your cameras catch that, too?"

Kristen slanted a look at Foley. He shrugged.

"What did the guy look like?" she asked, deciding it wouldn't hurt to play along.

"I don't know—average. About my age. Blondish hair, going gray, maybe, what there was of it. Not short, not tall." Morris's face twisted with frustration. "Go look at the video."

Kristen glanced at Foley again. He gave a little nod and slipped out of the room.

Kristen remained silent for a few minutes, deciding it wouldn't hurt to let Morris sweat a little more. She wasn't really buying his story about another man—what were the odds that there were two men, both with an axe to grind with Sam Cooper, collaborating on the threats against Maddy?

But might as well be thorough. Foley would check with Jefferson County Courthouse security and be back with the answer. Meanwhile, she could toy with Morris a little more, see if she could coax a confession out of him.

"You don't believe me, do you?" Morris broke the silence after a couple of minutes.

"Don't you think it's a bit of a coincidence that a guy who has it in for Sam Cooper managed to find the only other guy in town who feels the same way?"

"Maybe he heard about my son's case."

"And just knew you'd go along with his plan to terrorize Cooper?"

"I didn't know what he was going to do with the photos."

"Then why did you take them?"

"He said he was working for Cooper's old lady."

"His old lady?"

"Yeah, the kid's mother. Said she was looking to take the kid away from Cooper, and if I'd take pictures of her at the day care it would prove he just pawned her off every day to other people to take care of."

Kristen frowned. "Maddy Cooper's mother is not seeking custody of Maddy."

Morris looked confused. "She's not?"

"No, she's not."

He pressed his lips into a tight, thin line. "Then he lied to me about what he was up to."

"Isn't it more likely that you decided to pick this excuse for your own behavior without knowing the real situation between Sam Cooper and his ex-wife?" Kristen asked gently. "It's understandable, to assume Maddy's mother wanted custody. Most mothers do."

"You're trying to twist me up and make me cop to something I didn't do," Morris protested. "I didn't touch that kid. Or that girl, either." He pushed away the photo of Cissy. "I wouldn't do that."

Foley came back into the room. She looked up. He gave a small shake of his head.

"The camera outside the courthouse didn't pick up anyone else with you, Mr. Morris," she said aloud.

Morris looked up at her, alarmed. "He was there!"

"The camera didn't see him."

"I'm telling you—"

Foley pulled up a chair next to Darryl Morris, crowding close. "Mr. Morris, what say we start over from the beginning?"

"IS MOMMY REALLY GONE?" Maddy asked Sam that afternoon as he fed her a snack of peanut butter, banana and crackers.

He paused, his heart breaking a little for his daughter, who seemed more confused than saddened by the question. "She went back to Washington. That's where she lives, just like we did for a while, remember?"

Maddy licked a stray dollop of peanut butter from her fingers, blinking at him. "And she's not coming back?"

"Maybe now and then to visit. I don't know." He handed her a slice of banana. "Does that make you sad, baby?"

Maddy shook her head. "Now Miss Kristen can be my mommy, can't she, Daddy?"

He stared at her, nonplussed. "Miss Kristen isn't your mommy, Maddy Jane. You know that."

"But she can be, right? If I want her to?"

"I don't think it's that easy. Miss Kristen may not want to be your mommy."

The look of puzzlement on Maddy's face would have been comical under other circumstances. "Why not?"

"She may want to wait and have a little girl of her own."

"She don't have to wait."

"But maybe she wants to."

The light of determination in Maddy's green eyes reminded him of his younger sister, Hannah, who'd never taken no for an answer without a fight. "You do it, Daddy. You tell her to be my mommy."

He couldn't help but laugh at the thought. "I *know* that won't work."

She reached out and cradled his face between her sticky hands, her expression serious. "Try, Daddy."

He swept her up into his arms, cracker crumbs and all. "Tell you what. Why don't you take a nap and we'll talk about this when you wake up?" He tickled her gently to distract her.

She squealed in his ear, half deafening him, but at least she dropped the subject of Kristen after that. The last couple of days with Norah had apparently taken some energy out of her, for she settled down to her nap without protest, drifting off before he'd finished half of *The Cat in the Hat*.

He tucked her in, his mind still worrying with her question about Kristen. Of all the women in the world, why had Maddy decided a kidphobic cop with a bleak and tragic past was the best candidate for motherhood? Hell, why was he himself thinking about taking their already-complicated relationship into dangerous new territory?

Anytime now, Kristen could call with the news that Darryl Morris was the guy behind the attack on Cissy. Then it would all be over.

Maybe instead of thinking so much about how to make their relationship with Kristen last beyond the end of the case, he should be thinking about how to close the book on the Kristen Tandy chapter of his life for good.

"JEFFERSON COUNTY'S BOOKING him," Carl Madison told Kristen after another fruitless hour of interviewing Darryl Morris. "We only have the threatening message to hold him on, and that happened in their jurisdiction."

Kristen didn't answer, frustration bubbling deep in her gut. He'd admitted to almost everything except the attack on Cissy and the threat, and he hadn't wavered a bit from his story about a mystery man pulling the strings. The story seemed crazy, but if Morris was lying, he was lying consistently.

"We'll tie him to the attack," Foley added when she remained silent. "He's got to be the one."

She wanted to believe it. Then Maddy Cooper would be out of danger and safe to return to a normal, happy life with Sam and the rest of his family.

And she could get out of their lives before anyone got hurt.

Carl pulled her aside as they walked down the hall toward the detective's office. "Dr. Sowell from

Darden left a message for you. He asked if you were still planning to visit the facility this afternoon."

Damn. She'd forgotten about her planned drive to Tuscaloosa. She glanced at her watch. Almost three o'clock. If she left now, she could be there by five-thirty.

On her way down to the parking lot, she called Dr. Sowell to make sure someone would be there to talk to her about the mysterious "Bryant Thompson." He promised to stick around until she arrived, so he was waiting for her when she got to Tuscaloosa. He guided her through the security checkpoint, where she had to relinquish her Ruger P95 pistol to the guard before following the doctor to his office.

Sowell pulled a grainy black-and-white photo from the top drawer of his desk and handed it to her. "This is the man who introduced himself as Bryant Thompson. Do you recognize him?"

She looked at the image. The surveillance camera apparently covered the small visitors' area from a position high on the wall, giving her a bird's-eye view of the entire room but not much in the way of details about anyone in the frame.

There were only three people in the photo—the mysterious Bryant Thompson, a uniformed guard standing nearby and a thin, frail woman dressed in a white gown and a darker robe, her hands folded in her lap.

Kristen's stomach gave a sickening lurch as she realized the woman in the photo must be her mother.

She was almost entirely unrecognizable, no longer the woman Kristen remembered. Though hospitalized for only fifteen years, she looked decades older, her formerly dark red hair now a dull gray bird's nest twisted up in a messy knot atop her head. Her cheeks were thin and sunken, her body stooped and frail.

Tears burned Kristen's eyes, catching her unprepared. She blinked them away, steeling herself against a flood of devastating memories.

Just look at the photo, she told herself firmly. *Study the man. You already know the woman.*

She forced her attention to the man sitting across from her mother. He had light-colored hair—blond? Gray? Hard to say, given the photo was in black and white. He seemed to be sitting very still, his hands on his knees. He wasn't leaning forward into her mother's space, as she might have expected from someone claiming to be there to help her. If anything, he seemed to be keeping a careful distance.

Beyond that, she could see only small, unimportant details about the mystery man. He wore light-colored slacks, not jeans, and a jacket that might be corduroy.

"What do you remember about the man?" she asked Dr. Sowell.

"Very little, I'm afraid. I saw him only in passing, as I had been called to an emergency elsewhere. The guard on duty may be the best person to ask, but he works the day shift so he left earlier. I can give him your phone number and ask him to call you if you like."

She frowned at the photo, impatient. She didn't want to wait for the guard to call her. She wanted this mystery over with now, so she could put it behind her and never have to come back to this place again.

"Did you ask my mother about the man who visited her?"

Sowell seemed surprised by the question. "No. I didn't think it would be appropriate to interrogate her when she'd done nothing wrong."

"At least not this time," Kristen muttered.

Sowell gave her a pitying look. "Of course."

Dread crept over her, greasy and pitch-black, as she realized the best way to get the answers she needed about Bryant Thompson was to go directly to the source. She'd avoided this moment long enough. Time to face the demons head-on.

"Dr. Sowell, I'd like to talk to my mother."

Chapter Twelve

Kristen waited, her heart racing, for the guard to bring her mother out to see her. The interview room was cold, the chair uncomfortable and the atmosphere utterly bleak. Appropriate, she thought, a bubble of hysterical laughter knocking at the back of her throat.

The door to the room opened with a loud rattle and the guard entered first, his bulk filling the doorway. Right behind him, her bony wrist encircled by the guard's beefy hand, Molly Jane Tandy shuffled into the room. Someone had cut and combed her hair since her earlier visit with the mystery man calling himself Bryant Thompson. It was almost completely gray now, chopped to chin length and hanging in stringy, frizzy strands.

A pale pink, shapeless gown covered her body from throat to shins, a dark green terry cloth robe draped over her thin arms and shoulders to combat the hospital's chilly air. No belt, of course.

She was forty-seven years old. She looked closer

to sixty-seven, her haggard face dry and lined. The bright blue eyes that had once danced with wicked charm were now rheumy and restless, darting about the visitor's room before finally settling on Kristen's face. Her mouth dropped open in a silent O and her eyes widened.

"Kristy," she said, her voice a hoarse creak.

The urge to run was almost more than Kristen could control. She wrapped her fingers around the edges of the chair seat beneath her, gritting her teeth until she found the control to speak. "Hello, Mother."

Molly hurried forward, her arm outstretched. Kristen felt her whole body recoil and almost collapsed with relief when the guard caught Molly's arm and halted her approach. He was gentle but insistent as he settled her in the chair across from Kristen.

It hadn't been obvious in the photo, but in person, she saw that the patient's chair was a safe distance from the visitor's chair, well beyond arm's reach. The chair's legs were bolted to the floor, and the guard bent to slide a leather cuff around her mother's right leg, keeping her safely secured to her seat.

The burly guard took a step back, flashing Kristen a sympathetic look. She supposed he knew all about Molly's crime and could guess just how hard it was for Kristen to be here.

Normally, she hated pity, but this time, she found

the guard's kind look to be a comfort. It made her feel less alone.

Less vulnerable.

"Mother, Dr. Sowell told me that a man came to visit you the other day. He called himself Bryant Thompson."

"A lovely man," Molly said distractedly. "He spoke very well of you, Kristy."

"He spoke of me?"

Molly smiled. "Oh, yes. He told me that you're very important now. A policewoman." Her eyes brightened, the look in them almost beatific.

Kristen glanced at the guard. His eyes were on her mother, watchful and full of pity.

"Mother, did Mr. Thompson offer to do anything for you?"

"No, he only wanted to show me the picture."

"What picture?"

Her mother slowly reached into the pocket of her robe. Immediately the guard moved forward, stepping between Kristen and Molly. But his watchfulness was unnecessary; all Molly pulled from her pocket was a folded piece of paper. The guard took it from her, unfolded it, then handed it to Kristen.

It was a clipping from the *Chickasaw County Herald* newspaper, dated two days earlier. The article was about the break-in at Sam Cooper's home and the injury to his niece. There was a photograph accompanying the article, a telephoto shot of Kristen, Sam and Maddy in the chairs at the hospital. There must have been a reporter there with a digital camera, she realized, or a staff member who'd seen the chance to sell a newsworthy photo to the local rag.

"Mr. Thompson said you're watching out for that sweet little girl, Kristy. Is that true?"

Kristen dragged her gaze from the newspaper clipping. "Why would Mr. Thompson bring this to you?"

"He said it would be good for my recovery to know that you were doing so well," Molly answered. "And you know, I think it is. I feel so much better now, knowing that I have a chance to start over again."

Kristen narrowed her eyes, not following her mother's logic. "Start over again how?"

"With the little girl, of course," Molly said. Her tone of voice sounded calm and reasoned, though the light shining in her blue eyes was sheer madness. "Now that you're taking care of the little girl, you can bring her to see me."

Kristen stared at her in horror, realizing what her mother was suggesting. "No—"

"I could help you take care of her. I could teach you how to be a mother. I miss my own sweet babies so."

The guard made a low, groaning sound deep in his chest. Kristen looked up to find his face contorted with sheer horror.

Her own stomach had twisted into a painful knot,

bile rising to the back of her throat. She pushed out of her chair, throwing a pleading look at the guard.

"Outside to the right, third door on the left."

She bolted down the hall to the restroom, barely making it inside one of the stalls before she threw up.

She wasn't sure how long she remained in the bathroom stall, gripping the side of the toilet as she waited out the last of the dry heaves. Apparently it was long enough for the guard to have returned her mother to her room and contacted Dr. Sowell, for a few minutes later there was a knock on the door, and Dr. Sowell's concerned voice sounded through the heavy wood.

"Are you all right, Detective Tandy?"

She pushed herself up and flushed the toilet. "I'm okay," she called hoarsely, staggering slightly as she went to the sink to wash her hands and face. The woman staring back at her in the mirror looked like a war survivor, pale and haunted.

When she emerged from the restroom, the psychiatrist was waiting for her outside, his expression full of concern. "Hastings told me what happened. I'm sorry. I had no idea she'd ambush you that way."

Kristen shook her head. "I knew seeing her would be difficult after all this time. I'm fine."

"Is there someone I could call for you?"

"No, I'm okay. I just—I need to get out of here."

He walked her out to her car. He reached into his jacket pocket and pulled out a photo print. "You almost forgot this."

It was the photograph of the mysterious Bryant Thompson, sitting in the interview room with Kristen's mother. Kristen had left it on Dr. Sowell's desk, planning to return there before she left the facility.

She put it in her coat pocket with the clipping she'd taken from her mother. "Thank you. Let me know if my mother receives any other visits from this Bryant Thompson character."

"I will."

She settled behind the steering wheel of the Impala, breathing deeply to calm her still-ragged nerves. Her mouth tasted bitter; she dug in the glove compartment for a pack of breath mints she kept there and popped one in her mouth. As she started the car, she pulled the newspaper clipping from her pocket. Earlier, she'd noticed something bleeding through the back of the clipping. She turned it over now and found a ten-digit phone number written in black ink.

Her own cell phone number.

She rubbed her burning eyes, her mind spinning in a million different directions. Who was this man who called himself Bryant Thompson? What did he want from her mother?

And how the hell had he gotten her cell phone number?

SAM HAD JUST PUT MADDY to bed around eight-thirty that evening when he heard a knock on the guesthouse door. He finished tucking her in and dropped a kiss on her cheek. "Sleep tight, Maddycakes."

Already drowsing, she made a soft murmuring noise and rolled onto her side.

He went to the front door, opening it a crack to find Kristen Tandy on his doorstep, looking pale and tense.

"What's wrong?" he asked, letting her in. "Why didn't you just let yourself in with the key?"

She made an attempt to straighten her face. "Forgot I had a key." She sat on the sofa hunched forward, her elbows resting on her knees as if she was winded.

He sat beside her, alarmed by the obvious distress she was trying to hide. "I talked to Detective Foley a couple of hours ago. He said Morris hasn't confessed to the attack yet."

"He still looks good for it," she said, but he sensed a little hesitation underlying her words.

"But?"

She shook her head. "I don't know. It's—it's stupid. Every perp nabbed red-handed tries out the same lame excuse—'I didn't really do it. You have the wrong guy.'"

"Foley said he admitted most of it."

"He admitted delivering the envelope. He admitted taking the photos. But he said someone paid him for them, and he didn't know what they were for. He also swears he didn't write the threatening note on the back of the photo."

"Do you believe him?"

She paused, the furrow in her brow deepening. "Morris admits holding you responsible for dropping the charges against the man who hit his son's motorcycle. He cops to the taking the pictures. But we're supposed to believe someone else asked him to take them and deliver them to you? It's crazy." Her voice firmed up. "It's unbelievable. He's got to be the guy."

"So it's over?" Sam was afraid to believe.

"I think so," she said after a pause.

"Who's booking him? Chickasaw County or Jefferson?"

"All anyone can book him on at the moment is the threatening note to you. That happened in Birmingham, so Jefferson County's going to file the charges for now. But we're still trying to tie him to the attack on Maddy and Cissy."

"They won't let me near the case." He smiled wryly. "You'll probably have to give me all the updates."

She slanted a look at him, her expression almost pained.

"Okay, that's it," he said. "What's wrong?"

She looked away. "Nothing."

"It's not nothing."

She pushed to her feet. "It's been a long day and I could use a shower and some sleep. Let's table this until morning."

He stood, closing his hand around her upper

arm. She looked up at him, her eyes wide and dark with pain.

He eased his grip on her arm. "You're scaring me."

She looked away. "It's nothing to do with Maddy or this case. It's personal."

He moved his hand slowly up her arm, over her shoulder, finally settling his fingers gently against the soft curve of her cheek. He lifted his other hand to cradle her face between his palms, forcing her to look at him. Her lips trembled as she visibly fought for control.

"Tell me what happened," he said in a quiet but firm voice.

She closed her eyes. "Sam, please. Just let it go, okay?"

He let go with reluctance, stepping back. She opened her eyes, gave him a halfhearted smile and went down the hall to the bathroom, leaving him to lock up for the night.

He checked the doors and windows, tiptoeing into Maddy's room to double-check the window by her bed. Outside, the moon had risen high in the cloudless sky, surrounded by a million stars. He'd forgotten, living in D.C., what the night sky looked like when there weren't a lot of city lights around to pollute the view.

He heard the shower kick on down the hall, and he left Maddy's room quietly, his mind returning to the disturbing encounter with Kristen. What had set her on edge that way? Knowing what he did of her past, he imagined it would take something pretty terrible to shake Kristen Tandy's control.

He suddenly remembered her shaken reaction to the phone call she received the day before. What had he heard her say to the caller?

Tell her no.

Tell whom no? Had to be her mother, didn't it? Who else could send Kristen into such an emotional tailspin?

It's none of your business, Cooper.

The case was nearly over. Morris was in jail, waiting for arraignment. With any luck, the judge would deny bail and Sam and Maddy could go back to a normal life, while Kristen Tandy went on to whatever case came her way next. It was better for everyone that way, he told himself.

But he knew letting Kristen walk away wasn't going to be anywhere near that simple or easy.

A hot metallic odor permeated the air as Kristen bent over the trash can in the kitchen and tried to throw up, though her stomach was empty after a long night's sleep. She welcomed the pain of the dry heaves, needing something to crowd out the pictures imprinted on her brain.

Blood everywhere, smeared on the walls and floor, spread over the bedsheets and the pajamas and nightgowns of her younger brothers and sisters—the images burned into her brain. Kristen had found Tammy first, her nine-year-old sister's small body stretched out on the floor in the hall outside Kristen's bedroom, half blocking the door. She'd crouched by her sister, her mind rebelling against what she was seeing, only to realize there was more blood. A lot more blood.

Four bodies. Julie. Tammy. David. Kevin. All beyond help. And her mother was nowhere to be found.

The dry heaves ended and she slithered to the floor, tears sliding silently down her cheeks. She tried to think. What should she do? Who should she call now?

"Kristy?" Mama's voice was soft and bewildered.

Kristen looked up. Mama stood in the kitchen doorway, still in her pale blue night-gown. Blood painted a grotesque abstract pattern across the nylon fabric. She held a large chef's knife at her side. Blood dripped from the blade to the linoleum in slow, steady drops.

Kristen's heart slammed into her rib cage.

Mama walked past her to the sink. She laid the knife on the counter and reached for the paper towels hanging on the wall by the stove. On one of the eyes, a pot of oatmeal was boiling over, making a mess on the stovetop.

Mama wet a couple of paper towels under the tap and wiped up the overflow. Pulling open the utensil drawer, she pulled out a steel serving spatula, shaped like a diamond with a fleur-de-lis cutout in the middle, and started stirring the oatmeal.

Kristen stared at the spatula, her overloaded brain latching on to that one small incongruity. Why would Mama use a cake spatula to stir oatmeal? That was crazy.

Mama turned to look at her, her eyes widening as if she were surprised to see Kristen. "When did you get up, baby?"

Kristen stumbled backward. "I need to go get dressed."

"Have breakfast first." Mama scraped the spatula on the edge of the pan. "It's almost ready. Go get yourself a bowl."

Afraid to disobey, Kristen crossed to the cabinet next to the stove, her knees shaking, and retrieved a plastic cereal bowl. She started to set the bowl down beside her mother, but Mama grabbed her hand, leaving a smear of blood on Kristen's wrist.

"Hold it still while I scoop." Mama's voice was unbearably calm. Kristen's hand shook as Mama scooped up hot oatmeal with the spatula. Chunks of hot cereal spilled through the fleur-de-lis cutout, splashing on Kristen's hand.

"Ow!" She tried to jerk her hand away but Mama's grip tightened.

"Why are you such a big baby?" Her

mother's voice rose hysterically. She shoved the pan off the eye and set the spatula down over the flame. Oatmeal caught fire and burned to carbon, blackening the spatula.

"Mama, no—"

"Miss Kristen?"

The tiny voice caught her by surprise. She looked away from the madness in Mama's eyes and saw Maddy Cooper standing in the kitchen doorway, dressed in blue Winnie the Pooh pajamas and carrying a battered gray stuffed raccoon.

"Maddy—" Terror gripped her, crushing her heart until she could barely feel it beating. She had to get Maddy out of here, away from Mama, before—

Pain seared the back of her hand. She cried out and turned to look at Mama. But Mama was looking at Maddy, a gleam of excitement in her mad blue eyes.

"You brought her to see me, Kristy. Just like I asked."

Kristen pulled her aching hand away and grabbed for the knife. But Mama reached it first.

Kristen threw herself in front of Maddy, covering the child with her whole body.

"No, Mama. Please!"

Maddy wriggled against her. "Miss Kristen, wake up!"

KRISTEN JERKED AWAKE, her heart scampering like a jackrabbit in her chest. A shaft of light poured in from the half-open door, illuminating the dim room.

And her arms were wrapped tightly around a flailing Maddy Cooper.

Chapter Thirteen

Kristen loosened her grip, and Maddy looked up at her, a comical look of surprise on her face. "You squeezed too tight!"

"I'm sorry, sweetie." She stroked Maddy's hair, relief washing over her in enervating waves. "I must have been dreaming. What are you doing here?"

Maddy cuddled close, her sweet baby scent enveloping Kristen, as tangible as a touch. "I heard you crying. I brought Bandit to make you feel better." She held up the well-worn plush raccoon that was her favorite toy, as Kristen had quickly learned.

Kristen kissed the little girl's warm forehead, closing her eyes against the lingering images of her nightmare. She could still feel the bone-deep pain of the burn on the back of her hand, but she ignored it. It was a phantom, long gone.

Right here, right now, she was safe. And so was Maddy.

Footsteps sounded in the hallway, and Sam

Cooper's tall, broad body filled the doorway. He wore only a pair of black silk boxer shorts and a white T-shirt that he'd apparently just thrown on, if the twisted fabric was anything to go by.

"Everything okay?" he asked, his blue eyes dark with worry.

"Everything's fine," she assured him.

He entered the bedroom. "Maddycakes, time to get back in your bed."

"Let her stay a little longer," Kristen blurted, as surprised by the words as Sam seemed to be.

"Are you sure?"

"I'm sure." Maddy was already starting to get drowsy-eyed. She'd be asleep in no time, and Kristen could take her back to her bed. Right now, however, she needed to feel Maddy's warm little body tucked safely next to her to drive away the last, lingering wisps of her nightmare.

"I'll take her back to her bed when she falls asleep," she added softly when Sam made no move to leave the bedroom.

He hesitated a moment longer, his gaze appraising. "Okay," he said finally. "Night again, Maddycakes."

"Night, Daddy!" Maddy snuggled closer to Kristen.

Kristen watched Sam leave, understanding his reluctance. She hadn't given him much reason to trust her maternal instincts, and he had to be worrying that Maddy would get hurt in the long run.

Kristen had worried about that herself, knowing

that the child was already becoming attached to her. But the case would be over soon—possibly was over already, if they could tie up all the loose ends of the case against Darryl Morris. Then she'd move to another case and be out of Sam's and Maddy's lives for good.

Hot tears hammered at the back of her eyes at the thought of saying goodbye to them, but she fought the emotion, knowing a clean break was the right thing to do, no matter how painful. If her visit with her mother had done anything, it had convinced Kristen that she'd been right all these years to avoid motherhood as though it was a disease.

Except *she* was the disease, not motherhood. She was the one with insanity in her genes and a maternal role model wretched enough to make the very notion of having children an unbearably bad risk.

"Miss Kristen, do you know any songs?" Maddy's sleepy voice pulled her out of her bleak thoughts.

She pasted on a smile. "I'm not much of a singer. Why don't you start, and if I know the song, I'll sing along."

"Okay!" Maddy smiled and propped herself up against Kristen's arm. She thought a moment, then started singing "Old McDonald Had a Farm." By the time they got to the sillier farm animals, Kristen found herself laughing as hard as Maddy.

"Okay, next one's gotta be a lullaby, bug," she told Maddy as the little girl's giggles finally subsided. She put her arm around Maddy and tucked her close. A tune from the distant past drifted into her mind, a reminder of a simpler, sweeter time. As Maddy snuggled against her, she started singing.

"River rolls closer, near the green hills. Reaches for the moon, but the moon stands still. Moon stands still while the river runs, waiting in the dark for Mr. Sun."

Maddy's eyes closed as Kristen repeated the same verse, the only one she could remember. It had been a silly song she'd made up to sing Julie to sleep. She'd forgotten it until just now, maybe because she'd spent so much time trying to forget the horrors of that last day with her brothers and sisters that she'd buried the good memories, too.

Maddy drifted off to sleep just as a flood of emotions started to break through the fortifications Kristen had built up in her mind over the last fifteen years. A hundred images swam through her thoughts, for the first time in a long time more sweet than bitter. Blinking back tears, she picked up Maddy and carried her back to her room, settling her under the covers.

Maddy turned over, her sweet face burrowing into her pillow. Kristen felt a smile breaking through her sadness as she slipped from the room, closing the door behind her.

"She asleep?"

Sam's voice, emerging from the darkness of the

hallway, was a shock to her system. She pressed her hand over her chest, acutely aware that she hadn't even bothered to throw on a robe over the tank top and silk shorts she'd worn to bed.

"Yes," she answered, starting to sidle past him to her room. But he caught her arm, keeping her in place. Sparks ignited along her spine, radiating out from where his big, warm hand closed over her bare arm.

"Good," he said. "Because we need to talk."

She eyed him warily. "About what?"

"About where you went this afternoon." Sam caught her chin, forcing her gaze up to meet his. "You went to see your mother, didn't you?"

Her heart skipped a beat. "What makes you think that?"

"Carl Madison called to check on you while you were in the shower. He was worried he couldn't get you on your cell phone and wondered if seeing your mother again had been too much for you." Sam ran his thumb over the curve of her chin. "Was it?"

Kristen glanced at Maddy's bedroom door. "Do we have to talk about this tonight?"

He dropped his hand. "Not if you don't want to."

She threw him an exasperated look, hating how much she wanted to tell him everything she'd been through that day. Right now, a pair of warm, strong arms wrapped around her seemed like the most necessary thing in the world.

She settled for admitting, "I didn't think I wanted to."

"But now you do?"

She made a growling noise deep in her throat and walked away, heading for the darkened living room. Her shin made contact with the end table by the sofa, sending pain shooting up her leg. She uttered a quiet, heartfelt curse and fumbled for the lamp switch. A twist of the knob later, lamplight flooded half the room, illuminating the sofa.

With a sigh of surrender, Kristen turned to look at Sam. "A couple of days ago, my mother's doctor called Carl, asking for me. He told Carl my mother wanted to see me."

"And Carl called you," Sam guessed correctly. "That was the call you took the day Norah arrived, right? The one that had you so upset."

She briefly considered arguing with him about his assessment of her mood that day, but he was right. The call had scared the hell out of her, among other things.

She slumped onto the nearest sofa cushion, wrapping her arms around herself. "I told Carl I didn't want to see her."

"I remember."

She licked her lips. "But the doctor called me today."

Sam sat beside her, careful to leave her plenty of space, she noticed bleakly. Apparently she was giving off major "don't touch" vibes.

"Is it the first time you've seen her since she was committed?" he asked gently.

She met his curious gaze, her lips twisting in a wry smile. "Yeah. Probably the last, too."

"Why did you decide to see her after all this time?"

She supposed it wouldn't hurt to tell him about Bryant Thompson. She reached for the jacket she'd left draped over the arm of the sofa and pulled the clipping from the pocket. "Because of this."

Sam frowned as he took in the article. "I thought you said it wasn't related to the attempted kidnapping."

"I don't think it is. Someone visited my mother yesterday, out of the blue. He brought her this photo."

Sam looked puzzled. "Who would do that? And why?"

"That's what I'm going to have to find out." She took back the clipping and put it in her pocket. "But that's my mystery, not yours." The last thing she wanted to do was involve Sam in her life any more than he was already, not when she was on the verge of walking away for good.

A clean break would be better for everyone, right?

"You helped me with mine. Maybe I could help you with yours," he offered.

She had to smile at the offer. "How do you plan to do that, Sherlock?"

He brushed a lock of hair away from her cheek. Her smile faded, replaced by a tremble in her lips that had nothing to do with fear and everything to do with the crackling heat simmering low in her belly. "Maybe we could start with why seeing your mother after all this time bothered you so much," he murmured.

She grimaced, trying not to lean any closer to him. "That's not really a mystery, is it?"

"Do you ever talk about what happened to you?"

She shook her head. "Not if I can help it."

"But you still think about it."

"Every day." She sighed. "Look, Sam, I appreciate what you're trying to do here. But there are some things I can't—" She broke off with a wince, unable to find the words.

In his eyes, she saw his internal struggle. He wanted to help her—she saw the urge so clearly that she found herself feeling sorry for him. Poor Sam, trying to break through a decade and a half of walls she'd built to protect herself, she thought. She loved him a little bit for it, even though she wasn't sure she'd ever let those walls fall completely.

Silence stretched between them, taut and uncomfortable. Kristen closed her fingers around her knees, squeezing tightly as she struggled against the tears burning behind her eyes. She felt words hammering the back of her throat, struggling to find a voice, but she had no idea what to say.

When she finally opened her mouth and let the words spill out, they were the last thing she expected. "My mother asked me to bring Maddy to see her."

"What?"

She turned to look at him, hating herself for putting that look of horror on his face. "Forget it. It doesn't matter. I'm not going to see her again."

"Why did she want to see Maddy? Why did she think you'd ever do such a thing?"

Kristen scraped her hair away from her face. "She's crazy, Sam. She looked at that newspaper clipping and that's what she got out of it. That I had access to your four-year-old daughter and I could bring Maddy by to see her."

She could see Sam floundering for a response to such madness. "How—what—?"

She gave a huff of brittle, mirthless laughter. "Yeah, my thoughts exactly." Her laughter died in her throat as the nightmare of her past swooped in like a vulture, feeding off her pain. "She said she missed her little ones so much."

Sam looked sick. "My God."

The tears she'd been fighting reached critical mass, spilling over her lower eyelids and trickling down her cheeks in hot streaks. "She thought—" She had to stop, swallowing hard before starting again, her voice low and choked. "She thought I'd bring Maddy there to her because she missed her babies. The babies she stabbed to death and left bleeding where they lay." She broke off with a soft, bleating sob.

"Oh, honey." Sam wrapped his arm around her, pulling her close. She turned, burying her face against his throat, needing the warm, solid strength of his body against hers more than she'd expected.

She cried wordlessly a few seconds, then pulled back, wiping at the tears with her knuckles. "I don't know how much you know about what happened—"

"Just a few things people told me," he admitted.

"She'd always been, I don't know…scattered. Not very dependable. I don't really remember if she was always that way or if it just started after my father left us. I just know I was eight years old and suddenly I was the mommy of the household." She'd been so scared, as the days turned into weeks and she realized that her mother's little "spells" weren't going to go away. "I made lunch for the little ones, and if there were dishes to be washed or clothes to be laundered, I did most of that, too. Mama would do things if I asked her to, but she never seemed to think of them herself."

Sam made a low, murmuring sound of encouragement. "That must have been so hard for you."

She pushed her hair back from her damp face. "She kept telling me that I had to help her keep things together or the government would take us all away from her and split us up."

"There was nobody to look out for you and your brothers and sisters?" Sam asked, his voice unspeakably sad.

"My grandparents on my mother's side were dead, and I never had anything to do with my father's parents. I couldn't even tell you their names." She unclenched her fingers, flexing them in front of her. They felt cold and numb. "I did everything I could to keep the neighbors and our teachers from finding out how bad it was, because I was terrified the social workers would separate us." She gave another soft, defeated sob. "I should have let them. We'd all still be alive."

He shook his head. "You were a kid. You didn't know how bad it would get. Apparently nobody did."

"I should have gotten help for us. I should have—" She ended on a little noise of frustration, just as she always did when she thought about the past, about the mistakes she'd made. "I should have done something."

"You did. You took care of your brothers and sisters when nobody else did."

"I didn't protect them from the one thing I should have," she whispered. "I didn't protect them from her."

Sam took her hand in his, squeezing her fingers gently. "Whenever someone you love dies unexpectedly, you wonder what you could have done differently."

She shook her head, frustrated. "It's not the same—"

"Isn't it? My sister-in-law died eight years ago. Murdered. J.D. was in the navy at the time, away at sea. I know he wonders if being here instead would have changed things. My brother Gabe was late going to check on her when she called him with car trouble. He got there a few minutes after she was killed, just in time to find her body. He's still working through his guilt about that."

"They didn't know someone was going to kill her. But I knew my mother was insane."

"Insanity and murder are two different things, Kristen." He cupped her chin, his touch gentle but firm. "Your mother didn't abuse you physically, did she?"

She shook her head. Until the day she snapped, Molly Tandy's crimes against her children had been emotional rather than physical.

"Then how could you have known?"

"I just should have." She pulled away from his touch, not ready to be comforted. She'd spent too many years going over and over that day in her mind to be easily mollified by Sam's reasonable words. She stood up, rubbing her tired eyes. "It's late, Sam, and we've had a long day. Can't we table this for later?"

Sam looked inclined to argue, but she didn't give him a chance, heading down the hall toward the bedroom before he could speak. She closed herself inside the darkened room, pressing her ear to the door until she heard Sam's footsteps in the hall.

For a moment, the urge to fling the door open and invite him inside for the night was so tempting that she dropped her hand to the doorknob, making it rattle softly. Outside, Sam's footsteps halted, and she wondered if he'd heard the noise.

She heard the faintest sound, as if Sam had

placed his hand on the other side of the door. She leaned her head closer and imagined she could hear him breathing.

Was he leaning against the door the way she was? Did he want to come in as much as she wanted him to?

After a moment, she heard his footsteps move down the hall. His door opened and closed, and she slumped against the door, releasing a pent-up breath.

The one thing she couldn't afford was false hope for a life forever out of her grasp. Hot, sweaty sex with Sam Cooper might take her mind off her problems for a couple of hours, but nothing—and no one—could make her past disappear for good. Not even Sam and his beautiful little daughter.

The sooner she brought this case to an end, the better.

Chapter Fourteen

Kristen was dressed and on the phone when Sam walked into the guesthouse living room around 6:00 a.m. the next morning. She waved at the coffeepot on the counter and continued her conversation. "No, I agree. The evidence is pretty solid."

Sam poured a cup of coffee and leaned against the breakfast bar, taking advantage of a rare opportunity to watch Kristen without her paying attention. Though it was early Saturday morning, she was already dressed for work in a pair of charcoal trousers and a pale blue tailored blouse that did nothing to hide her sleek curves. As she turned to reach for a bowl in the cabinet by the sink, he caught sight of her waistband holster with her Ruger tucked inside.

The combination of feminine beauty and deadly firepower was unspeakably sexy, he thought with a grin.

Kristen tossed a glance over her shoulder, gesturing to the bowls in the cabinet. He nodded, and she pulled another one down for him.

"I'll be in the office around seven-thirty. See you then." Kristen closed her phone and dropped it in her trousers pocket.

"Foley?" Sam asked.

She nodded, handing him one of the bowls. "We're going to hand Darryl Morris over to the Birmingham Police this morning. A detective should be here around eight to transport him back to the city."

"Then I guess that means Maddy can go back to preschool Monday morning," he said, his relief palpable.

Kristen's brow furrowed. "I suppose that would be okay."

Her frown gave him an uneasy feeling. "You're not having doubts about Darryl Morris's guilt, are you?"

"No. He took the photos. He delivered them to your office. He's admitted that."

"And what about the man he claims paid him to do it?"

"There's no evidence such a man even exists," she answered firmly. "Morris has a grudge against you, and the things he's admitted to are pretty damning."

She was right. He knew she was. He was just leery about taking any chances with Maddy's safety.

But they had to start living a normal life again sooner or later. Putting Maddy back into preschool was a good first step. She'd be happy to see her friends again, he knew; she talked about them all the time.

He opened the cabinet under the cutlery drawer and peered at the cereal choices. His mother had stocked the pantry with entirely too many sugary choices, but he supposed that's what grandparents did with their grandchildren. In the back, he found a box of toasted wheat flakes. Reasonably nutritious.

He poured himself a bowl and flashed a questioning look at Kristen. She nodded and he poured a bowl for her, as well, before getting the milk out of the refrigerator.

"So now that you're about to go off bodyguard duty, what comes next for you?" he asked.

He heard a slight hesitation before she answered. "Foley will be continuing with follow-up on this case. He'll want to keep trying to tie Morris to the attack on Cissy. Maybe when she wakes up, she'll have more information."

"Foley? What about you?"

Kristen looked away, licking her lips. "Actually, I'm thinking about asking Carl to assign me to a different case."

A hot ache settled in the pit of Sam's gut. Even though he'd known she'd be going back to her own place sooner rather than later, he hadn't realized she was thinking about handing over the investigation to someone else.

"Why?" he asked.

She darted a quick look at him. "It's time to move on."

He didn't miss her meaning. "From Maddy and me, you mean."

A queasy expression darted across her face. "Don't you think that's for the best?"

"This is about the kiss, isn't it?"

She slanted another look at him. "You're fixated on the kiss, Sam. It was nothing. Hormones and stress."

"What about the rest of it?"

She pushed aside her untouched bowl of cereal with a growl of frustration. "The rest of what? What exactly do you think has been going on between us? We've known each other—what? Three days?"

"Sometimes that's all it takes," he said quietly, realizing how crazy he sounded. Why was he even arguing with her about this? Hadn't he already proved his judgment about women was pretty damned suspect? He'd been certain he and Norah were meant to be together, and look how well that had turned out.

"People like me don't get happily ever afters," Kristen said just as quietly, pain darkening her blue eyes.

It wasn't the response he'd expected. He'd figured she'd stick with how short a time they'd been acquainted, maybe toss in the fact that high-stress situations sometimes magnified emotions that wouldn't otherwise make a blip on a person's radar. They were good, sound arguments.

But she'd gone straight to the heart of the problem. She didn't believe they had a chance together because of her past. That's what it all came down to, wasn't it?

Well, he couldn't accept that argument. He couldn't accept that she was doomed to solitude because of her mother's sins. It wasn't right or fair.

He pushed aside his own cereal bowl, welcoming the surge of frustration that drove out the hurt he'd felt a few seconds earlier. "I know you had a horrible childhood. Your recent history probably hasn't been the greatest, either. But I don't think life picks winner or losers, Kristen. I think we choose that ourselves—if we have the guts to."

She stared at him, shaking her head. "You think the problem is that I'm afraid of being happy?"

"Yeah, I do."

She threw up her hands. "Believe me, I don't want to live alone the rest of my life. I don't want to freak out every time I'm around kids. I love kids! I used to be great with kids. I used to dream about growing up and having children of my own."

"Then do it."

She shot him a glare as he took a step toward her. He backed off.

"I would love to jump into a relationship with you and see where it goes. What woman wouldn't? You're sexy, successful, funny…." She drew a long, shaky breath, blinking hard to hold back the tears. "But I'm a bad risk, Sam. Not just for you but also for Maddy. My mother wasn't always crazy, you know. For all I know, what happened to her was genetic. It could happen to me, too."

"You can't know that."

"And you can't be sure I'm wrong," she countered.

He wanted to argue, but she was right. He couldn't be sure. He knew nothing about her mother's situation, what had caused her madness and whether or not Kristen's own mind was a ticking time bomb. "Have you never asked anyone what caused your mother's mental break? Her doctor, maybe?"

Her expression was bleak. "No."

"Maybe you should."

Her lips flattened with frustration. "I need to leave now. Before Maddy wakes up."

Sam swallowed hard, fighting the urge to touch her, to try something, anything to make her reconsider walking out of their lives this way. He could tell there was nothing he could say right now to change her mind.

He wasn't even sure he should try.

He stepped away from her, jamming his restless hands into his pockets. "Maddy will be hurt if you leave without saying goodbye, Kristen."

She grimaced. "It's been only three days, Sam. She'll forget me sooner than you think."

He wasn't so sure. Maddy had apparently reached the age where having a mother seemed important, and with her own mother heading back to D.C. and out of the picture, Maddy had picked Kristen to fill the void, just as she might have picked a new puppy at the pound.

Maybe Kristen was right not to make a big deal out of saying goodbye. Perhaps the best way to handle Maddy's certain disappointment would be the same way he'd handle saying no to a new puppy—blatant distraction tactics.

"I think you're right," he said evenly, even though a heavy ache had settled right in the center of his chest. "No big goodbye. I'll have my folks keep her busy today and tomorrow while I finish readying the house for us to move back, and Monday she'll start back to preschool, which she'll love. It'll be okay."

Kristen nodded, although he saw worry in her eyes. It was more than he'd seen in Norah's eyes when she left, he realized. All he'd seen in his ex-wife's expression as she headed for her gate at the airport were equal parts guilt and relief.

"This is for the best, Sam." Kristen reached for the bowl of now-soggy cereal sitting on the counter, starting toward the garbage disposal.

He caught her arm, stopping her. She gazed up at him, her lips trembling slightly.

It would be so easy to kiss her, he thought. Just a soft, sweet kiss goodbye.

But he forced himself to let her go, taking the bowl from her unsteady hands. "I'll take care of this. You should go now, before Maddy wakes up."

The stricken look in her eyes almost unraveled his resolve. But she moved away quickly, before he could falter, grabbing her purse and jacket and heading out the door at a clip.

Sam forced himself to empty the two bowls of cereal into the garbage disposal and wash up, needing the activity to take his mind off the strange, empty feeling that had hollowed out his insides the second the door had closed behind Kristen.

"WHEN I GET HOME, CAN WE go see Miss Kristen?" Maddy asked as Sam unlatched her safety seat Monday morning.

Sam sighed, lifting her out of the Jeep and setting her on the ground. "Miss Kristen is very busy at work now, Maddy. Don't you remember, we talked about this last night."

Maddy's little face scrunched up with displeasure. "I wanna see Miss Kristen!"

So much for his daughter being easily distracted. She'd been asking about Kristen for two days straight. "Tell you what, this afternoon, when Aunt Hannah picks you up from school, maybe she'll take you out fishing." He made a mental note to check with his sister to see if she already had a client lined up that afternoon. Surely she'd give herself a day or so to get settled back in from her trip to Arizona and wouldn't mind some one-on-one time with her youngest niece.

He saw warning signs that Maddy was gearing up

to argue, so he took her hand and tugged her gently up the walkway to the front entrance of Gossamer Ridge Day School, where the director, Jennifer Franks, was greeting children that morning. When she caught sight of Sam and Maddy, her expression shifted quickly to regret.

"I was horrified to read about Mr. Morris's arrest," she said earnestly. "I'm so sorry I hired him—we had no idea—"

"Nobody did," Sam assured her. "There was never any indication in his background that he'd be any sort of threat. You couldn't have known."

"Still, we take these things very seriously. We've hired guards to patrol the grounds during the day so parents can feel secure about leaving their children with us." Jennifer waved toward a young man in a blue uniform standing a few steps away. "One here at the front entrance and another in the play area."

Seeing the guard did ease Sam's mind a bit. He supposed the bad publicity about Morris had forced the director's hand.

Maddy caught sight of one of her friends and tugged her hand out of Sam's, dashing away with a squeal of delight. Sam watched her go with a smile, though mild anxiety tugged at his gut. Over the past few days, he'd gotten used to having her close, protected by himself or people he trusted implicitly. It was hard to let go of that control, but he couldn't keep her wrapped in cotton padding and stored under glass.

"She'll be fine," Jennifer said.

"She asked me to put her favorite stuffed toy in the bag," Sam warned the principal. "I know you have rules about bringing toys to school, but she's had a rough few days. I made her promise to give the backpack to the teacher as soon as she got in the classroom and not to bug Miss Kathy about taking Bandit out of the bag during class."

Jennifer smiled sympathetically. "I suppose we can look the other way just this once."

Sam thanked her, turning to watch Maddy until she disappeared into her classroom down the hallway. With a tugging sensation in the middle of his chest, he returned to his car to make the long drive into Birmingham for his first full day back at the office.

Sam was smart enough to know that any interference from him might jeopardize the District Attorney's case against Darryl Morris, and the last thing he wanted to do was provide Morris with any sort of get-out-of-jail-free card. So he resisted the temptation to snoop around the office's newest case, instead spending the morning buried under the backlog of cases he'd had to put on hold the week before while he dealt with the threat to Maddy, sorting through what cases could be easily pleaded out and which ones would require actual court time.

By the time his cell phone rang that morning around eleven, he was bleary-eyed and grateful for the interruption. "Cooper."

"Sam, it's J.D. Cissy's awake."

"JUST STICK WITH IT a few more days," Foley cajoled, following at Kristen's heels as she checked the fax machine to see if anything had come in overnight. She turned quickly, and Foley almost barreled into her, grabbing the file cabinet at the last second to stop his momentum.

"Stop following me around like a puppy," she ordered.

"Stop being a scaredy cat."

"Oh, that's mature." The fax machine tray was empty, so she edged around Foley and returned to her desk.

"It's not like you to turn your back on a case that's still active." Foley settled on the edge of her desk, in her way.

She shooed him off. "Park your backside on your own desk. And how would you know whether or not it's like me to turn my back on an open case? This was my first case as a detective."

Foley made a face. "You know what I mean. I saw how you tackled this case. You must want to see it through to the end. So why ask for reassignment? Unless you and Cooper—"

She glared at him. "Mind your own business, Foley."

He opened his mouth to respond, but the trill of his desk phone stopped him midsound. He slid off Kristen's desk and crossed to answer. "Foley."

Kristen straightened her desk blotter where Foley's hip had knocked it askew, wishing her fellow investigator wasn't quite so good a detective. He probably knew exactly why she'd asked Carl to assign her to a different case. And unlike Carl, who'd at least had the kindness to keep his comments to himself, Foley was likely to make her next few weeks miserable with his endless attempts at armchair psychoanalysis.

"We'll be there." Foley hung up the phone and picked up the folder in front of him. "Grab your jacket, Tandy. You're going to get to be in on the end of this case after all."

"What's going on?"

Foley stopped in the doorway, flashing a smile. "Cissy Cooper's awake. And she's talking."

"EVERYTHING SEEMS TO BE in proper working order," J.D. told Sam as they waited outside Cissy's hospital room for the nurse to finish taking her vital signs. "No neurological deficits or anything like that. She even remembers the night of the attack. When I told her the police had a suspect in custody, she said she thinks she can identify him if the police show her a photo."

Sam clapped his hand on his brother's arm, happy to see J.D. looking so relieved and excited. "This is the best news, huh? Did you call the police?"

"He did." Jason Foley walked up, followed closely by Kristen. Sam tried to make eye contact with her, but she kept her gaze on J.D.'s face, her expression impossible to read.

So that was how she thought she was going to play it, huh?

Like hell.

The nurse emerged, smiling at J.D. "You'd never know she was out for four days. She's doing really great, Mr. Cooper."

J.D. beamed at the nurse and headed back into Cissy's room. Foley and Kristen followed, and Sam brought up the rear, trying not to stare too obviously at Kristen's slim, curvy backside. Just two days away from her, and he felt like an addict twitching for the next hit.

Cissy looked good, Sam was relieved to see. She grinned weakly at him. "How's Maddy? Daddy said she didn't get hurt, but is she really okay?"

"She's fine," Sam assured his niece, squeezing her hand.

"Your father told us you remember the attack." Kristen moved closer to the hospital bed.

Cissy looked up at her. "I do."

Sam let go of Cissy's hand. "Cissy, this is Detective Kristen Tandy of the Gossamer Ridge Police Department."

He could see from the shift in his niece's expression that she recognized the name. But she didn't say anything, just held out her hand to Kristen. "Nice to meet you."

"I'm very happy to finally meet you, too," Kristen said with a smile. "This is Detective Foley. We've been investigating what happened to you. We picked up a suspect a couple of days ago—can you take a look at this picture?"

Kristen pulled a photograph from her notebook and handed it to Cissy, who brought the photo closer to her face.

Sam realized he was holding his breath. He let it go slowly, glancing from his niece to Kristen, whose expression was as tense as he felt.

Cissy handed the photo back to Kristen, her expression apologetic. "I'm sorry, no. That's not the guy."

Sam felt his chest contract into a painful knot. Kristen turned to look at him, her eyes bright with alarm.

"Where's Maddy?" she asked urgently.

"At school," Sam answered, his heart pounding.

"I'll drive," she said, and hit the door at a jog.

OUTSIDE TIME WAS MADDY'S favorite time of all. She liked coloring and singing and all the things she did with the teacher inside the school, but outside time was perfect. Just perfect.

Sometimes the teachers played games with them. Miss Kathy was the best at kick ball, and she laughed a lot. Maddy liked to hear Miss Kathy's laugh. It was a big, booming laugh, straight from her belly. Maddy sometimes tried to laugh just like that, although it came out kind of silly sounding. But that was okay. Daddy said it was okay to be silly sometimes.

Thinking about Daddy made her think about this

morning, when he'd told her that Miss Kristen was at work. Miss Kristen was a detective, Daddy said, and her work was Very Very Important. Maddy wondered what was important about being a detective. In fact, she wondered what a detective was, anyway.

She only knew that she liked Miss Kristen. She liked how Miss Kristen didn't try to treat her like a baby since she was a big girl now. She liked the sound of Miss Kristen's voice. And she liked Miss Kristen's smile, even though Miss Kristen didn't smile nearly as much as Aunt Hannah or Grand-mama. Maddy wondered why she didn't smile as much. *Maybe she needs a little girl to love,* Maddy thought. *Like me.*

Across the playground, a little girl screamed, and Maddy looked up with surprise. She saw Cassie Price jumping up and down shrieking, and a couple of the boys in her class had bent over to look at something in the grass.

Maddy saw Miss Kathy and Miss Debbie hurry over to see what was going on. She started across the playground, too, but a big hand reached out and stopped her.

She looked up and saw a tall man in a blue uniform standing just behind her. Her heart gave a little lurch of surprise.

"There's a snake over there," he said. Maddy thought his voice sounded familiar. He looked familiar, too, but she didn't know why. He had a big, bushy mustache and wore a pair of silvery sun-glasses. She could see herself in the glasses, she realized with a little smile.

"Come with me, Maddy. I'm taking you to your daddy."

Was he Daddy's friend? He had a uniform sort of like her Uncle Aaron's. Was he a policeman? "I'm not afraid of snakes," she said. Aunt Hannah had taught her how to handle the little green snakes that played around Grandmama's garden. She liked to feel their dry, scaly bodies wriggle through her fingers.

"But that's a poisonous snake," the man said firmly, taking her hand. She saw he had her backpack in his other hand. She could see the ringed tail of Bandit, her stuffed raccoon, hanging out of the zippered pocket.

The man saw her looking at the tail. He reached into the pocket and gave Bandit to her. She said thank you—Daddy said always say "please" and "thank you"—and hugged Bandit close, not liking the feel of the man's big hand around hers.

"Where's my daddy?" she asked aloud.

"He's waiting for you inside my van." The man pulled her toward the side gate of the playground fence. They had gone around the side of the school building, and Maddy couldn't see the other kids on the playground anymore.

The man opened the gate and gave her a little nudge to go through. He closed the gate behind them and pulled her hand.

Maddy looked at the van parked at the end of the small parking lot. It was green and looked old. There were two windows up at the front but no windows in the side. She didn't see Daddy inside.

"Where's my daddy?" she repeated, starting to feel scared.

The man opened the door of the van, picked her up and put her inside. He didn't even have a special seat for her, like Daddy did. Her legs dangled over the seat, and she felt hot tears on her cheeks.

"Where's my daddy?" she screamed, but the man had already closed the door. She saw him put something in her backpack and toss it into the bushes at the side of the building.

Maddy tried to open the door of the van to run away—Daddy said when you got scared, it was okay to run and find a grown-up you trusted—but she couldn't get it to open.

The man in the uniform opened the front door and pulled himself into the seat behind the steering wheel. He spoke to her, his voice firm. "No crying, Maddy. You have to be a big girl now, okay?" He pulled a cap from the dashboard and put it on. Maddy's eyes widened.

Now she knew why the man in the uniform looked and sounded familiar. He was the bad man.

The bad man who hurt Cissy.

Chapter Fifteen

Sam clutched the cell phone more tightly as Kristen swerved around slow-moving traffic on I-59. He was on interminable hold, waiting for the preschool's principal to come on the line. He'd made a call as soon as they got outside the hospital, but the principal had been out of the office and he'd had to leave a message. He'd spent the next twenty minutes certain that Jennifer Franks would return his call at any moment.

When she didn't, he called again. The principal still wasn't in her office, but this time, he told the secretary that he wasn't hanging up until he talked to her boss.

"Still nothing?" Kristen asked, sounding as annoyed as he felt. "You've been on hold forever."

Just then, there was a click on the other end of the line and Jennifer Franks's breathless voice greeted him. "So sorry, Mr. Cooper. We've had a bit of an uproar I've been trying to get under control."

Sam's stomach twisted. "What kind of an uproar?"

"One of the children found a rather large snake on the playground a little while ago. We're still trying to find out whether or not it's harmless, and several of the children are very upset. We've had to call some parents."

Sam tamped down his impatience. "I left a message with your secretary twenty minutes ago—I'm trying to locate Maddy. Did you get that message?"

"No, I'm sorry—my secretary just told me. Maddy's class was outside for recess when the snake incident happened, but Maddy wasn't one of the children involved."

"Where is she now?"

"I assume she's back in her classroom with her teacher."

"You assume?"

Across the seat, Kristen muttered a profanity under her breath.

"I'll check right now. Hold on a moment."

"I'm on hold again," Sam muttered.

"For God's sake!" Kristen jerked the wheel, taking the Impala around a slow-moving coal truck at breakneck speed. "How hard is it to find one four-year-old?"

"Mr. Cooper?"

The fear he heard in Jennifer Franks's voice made Sam's blood freeze. "Tell me you found her safe and sound," he said.

"I'm sorry. We don't know how it happened."

"What happened, damn it?"

Kristen shot him a look full of unadulterated terror.

"She didn't return with the rest of her class after recess," Jennifer answered, sounding sick. "We don't know where she is."

"Get your security guards to start searching every inch of the grounds."

"I've already sent my assistant out to do just that. I don't think we should panic yet, Mr. Cooper. It's possible that she was there for the snake incident and ran away to hide because she was scared."

He wished he could believe that, but he knew that snakes didn't scare Maddy. He'd actually had to give her a lesson on not touching snakes unless a grown-up was there to supervise, for fear she'd end up trying to befriend a ground rattler or one of the bigger copperheads that roamed the woods near the lake.

"Please call me back with any news. I'm on my way."

"Should we contact the police?"

"I'll handle that," Sam answered, ringing off only long enough to dial his brother-in-law's cell phone number. A few moments later, Hannah's husband answered. "Deputy Patterson."

"Riley, it's Sam. Maddy's missing from her preschool and I'm about thirty minutes out. I need you to go there and supervise the search if you can."

"Of course. What can you tell me?"

He outlined for his brother-in-law what Jennifer

Franks had told him. "You know Maddy—a snake wouldn't have scared her away. I'm afraid the man who tried to take her before may have gotten to her this time."

"I thought Jefferson County had the guy in custody."

"They have Darryl Morris in custody—but Cissy just woke up from her coma. She said Morris definitely isn't the guy who attacked her."

"Son of a bitch," Riley growled. "Did she give you a description of who we *are* looking for?"

"I left as soon as I heard Morris wasn't the guy. Detective Foley with the GRPD is still there taking her statement. Right now, we're just looking for Maddy."

"I'm about five minutes away from the preschool," Riley said. "I'll call you in a few." He rang off.

Sam snapped his cell phone shut. "This isn't happening."

"This is my fault," Kristen muttered, white-knuckling the steering wheel through the interstate traffic. "I knew in my gut Morris was too easy an answer, but I wanted to believe it was over."

"We all did," Sam said firmly. The last thing Kristen needed to do was second-guess herself now, when she needed to focus. "Don't kick yourself. The evidence was there. We just didn't know there were missing pieces."

"Except Morris told us all along there was someone else involved," Kristen said, her tone full of disgust. "I should have looked deeper."

"You will now."

She released a shaky breath, and for the first time Sam realized she was hovering on the edge of tears. "I'm so sorry, Sam. I never should have agreed to let Carl put me in charge of protecting Maddy. I knew it was a bad idea."

"If you'd still been with Maddy, she wouldn't be missing," Sam replied. "You wouldn't have taken your eye off her for even a second. So stop blaming yourself. We all thought she was out of danger." He touched her shoulder. "I need you with me on this. I need your focus. Tell me you can do that."

She spared him a quick look. "I can do that."

They had reached their exit on the Interstate. They'd be at the school in ten minutes. Sam tried to keep his mind away from worst-case scenarios. The snake might not have scared Maddy, but she'd shown a hearty self-protective streak over the past few days, hiding first from the kidnapper and then from her mother when she'd felt threatened by Norah's careless comments.

"Could she be hiding?" Kristen asked, her mind moving in tandem with his. "I know the snake wouldn't have scared her, but maybe all the commotion spooked her?"

"Maybe." He was afraid to hope. His gut was telling him it wouldn't be that easy. Not this time.

Kristen killed the sirens about a block from the preschool. "The kids'll be freaked out enough as it is."

He slanted a look at her, wondering how she could possibly believe she wasn't mother material. Even with all the uncertainty about Maddy's whereabouts, Kristen had enough presence of mind to worry about the other children.

He hadn't even given them a thought.

Riley Patterson was waiting for them at the front of the school, easy to spot thanks to his signature pearl-gray Stetson, a legacy of his native Wyoming. Sam could tell by the look on his brother-in-law's face that the news wasn't good.

"We've found her backpack in the bushes near the side gate." Riley's voice was tight. "And one of the security guards is missing."

"Missing?" Sam frowned at Riley. "You think someone got rid of him to get to Maddy?"

"We're not sure," Riley said. "There's no sign of a struggle, no blood or anything like that—"

"Where's the backpack?" Kristen asked. She'd already pulled on a pair of latex gloves.

Riley gestured for them to follow. "I wanted to wait until you got here to take a look at it. You'd know what's missing, if anything." He led them around the side of the building, where a yellow barrier tape flapped lazily in the warm midday breeze. A handful of people from the neighborhood had gathered outside the fence, watching curiously as Sam, Kristen and Riley approached the backpack lying on its side near the bushes.

Sam felt moisture burning his eyes as he saw

Maddy's name written in faded denim letters stitched to the side of the backpack. Hannah had made those letters for Maddy out of a pair of old jeans and let Maddy help her stitch them to the bag.

His whole family had pitched in when he returned home to Alabama with his little girl, knowing how much harder her life was going to be without a mother there for her full-time. If something had happened to his baby—

Kristen's warm hand slipped into his. He looked down at her and found her gazing up at him with scared blue eyes. But her jaw was squared and mingled with the fear was a bracing double shot of determination.

"Focus on the evidence," she said. "You packed the bag for her this morning, right? Tell me if something's missing."

He squeezed her hand, grateful for her calming presence. He hunkered down with her as she crouched beside the backpack, watching her carefully open the bag to look inside.

"Bandit's missing," he said aloud, noticing the stuffed raccoon's absence immediately. Maddy's favorite toy had taken up most of the space in the bag.

"Her stuffed raccoon," Kristen explained when Riley gave Sam a querying look. "She's very attached." She pulled the zipper down farther. There was a small gold change purse inside—empty, since Maddy had no concept of money. She only liked the little purse because of its shiny color.

Kristen picked up the purse, looking at it, her eyes damp. Sam put his hand on her back, and she shot him a grateful look. Putting the purse down, she opened one of the outside pockets. "Commander Patterson, do you have tweezers or something like that?"

"What is it?" Sam asked as Riley reached into his pocket and brought out a slim, leather-bound tool kit.

"It looks like a piece of paper." Kristen took the tweezers Riley gave her and reached into the zippered pocket to withdraw a small piece of paper folded into four sections. Using the tweezers and the very tip of her gloved finger, she nudged the paper open.

There was writing inside, blocky letters just like the ones Sam had found on the back of the photos Darryl Morris had delivered to the D.A.'s office.

"'Let's make a deal,'" Kristen read aloud, her voice shaking. "'Your life for hers.'"

Riley muttered a soft string of curses.

"What kind of sick game is this guy playing?" Kristen dropped the note into the clear plastic bag Riley had produced from his jacket pocket and started going through the other pockets with greater urgency, as if hoping she'd find something that would contradict the message she'd just discovered.

"I don't think it's a game," Sam said thoughtfully, his initial fear beginning to subside. At least he could be pretty sure his daughter was still alive, if the man was talking about a trade. The fact that Bandit was missing also gave him hope; only someone who cared about Maddy's emotional state would have bothered dragging the stuffed toy along with them.

Whoever had taken Maddy wanted her alive, as a pawn in his game, not as a victim. It wasn't great news, but Sam would take it. It was a hell of a lot better than finding his daughter's body under the bushes instead.

Riley put his hand on Sam's shoulder. "I'm going to call this in and get a few more deputies down here. I'll see if the DEA can spare Aaron, too."

Sam stood and shook Riley's hand. "Thanks, man. Call Hannah, too. She needs to let the rest of the family know what's going on."

As Riley went to make the radio call, Sam turned to Kristen. "Was there anything else in the backpack?"

Kristen shook her head. "That was it."

"So he's going to find a way to get in touch with me."

Kristen pulled her gloves off and planted herself in front of him. "You're not making a trade, Sam."

"You can't stop me."

She moved even closer, her gaze locked with his. "If you try to make the deal, you're just playing his game."

"It's the only game in town, Kristen." He laid his hands on her shoulders, running his thumbs gently over the curve of her collarbone. "I will do anything for my daughter. Including die for her, if it comes to that."

"I know that. But we can't be stupid about this."

"What am I supposed to do?" He felt some of his control begin to slip. "That man has my daughter. He holds all the cards here. We're practically at square one now that Cissy's eliminated Morris as a suspect."

"No, we're not." Kristen closed her hands over his, her fingers warm and strong. "Cissy is giving Foley a description as we speak. And, you know, Darryl Morris may have been telling the truth about his accomplice. We may be able to get more information from him."

Something that had been niggling at the back of Sam's mind since he'd arrived at the preschool snapped into focus. "The missing guard," he said.

Kristen's brow creased for a second, then smoothed with a look of understanding. "The guard took Maddy."

Sam nodded, his mind racing. "I've taught her about being wary with strangers, but she knows that someone in uniform is a person who can help her when she's in trouble."

"He used the snake situation as a distraction," Kristen added. "Maybe he even engineered it himself."

"And he was already in place, in a position of trust. Nobody was going to think twice about a security guard leading Maddy away from the confusion." Sam shook his head. "How did he ever get a job here?"

"Maybe he doesn't have any sort of record." Kristen looked around, catching sight of Riley returning to the taped-off crime scene. "Deputy, can you keep an eye on the scene? We need to talk to the teachers and kids."

Riley slipped under the tape. "Sure. I've got some men on the way. Aaron's out of pocket," he added, speaking to Sam, "but I left a message with the DEA for him."

"Thanks," Sam said, hurrying to catch up with Kristen, who was already halfway to the school entrance.

"HERE'S A PHOTOCOPY OF HIS driver's license," Jennifer Franks said, looking about ten years older than she had the last time Kristen had seen her, the day she'd answered questions about Darryl Morris. She handed the paper to Kristen.

"Grant Mitchell," she read aloud, studying the grainy photo. Driver's license photos were almost never flattering, and this one was no exception. The man in the photo was in his late forties or early fifties, with short-cropped brown hair and a handlebar mustache that made him look like a throwback to the Civil War era. The photocopy wasn't the best quality, so it was impossible to make out much about the man's eyes, nor could she read anything in his expression that might give her a clue to the man inside.

Though she was sure she'd never met the man before, he seemed vaguely familiar to her. She showed Sam the photocopy. "Anyone you know?"

He studied the paper, his brow creased with concentration. After a moment, he released a disappointed sigh. "No, I don't think so." He looked across the desk at Jennifer. "Is this photo a good likeness?"

"Drivers' licenses never are," Jennifer said. "But yes, I'd say that's what he looks like, more or less."

"This doesn't make sense," Sam muttered.

Kristen laid her hand on Sam's shoulder. "Maybe we're wrong about Grant Mitchell. He could be a victim here, too. Or maybe he just decided guarding preschoolers isn't for him." She took the photocopy from Sam and looked down at the driver's license. "We could try his address—"

She stopped, rereading the address listed on the license. 1240 Copperhead Road. She slumped in her seat. "This address doesn't exist," she told Sam, showing him the photocopy. "There's no 1240 Copperhead Road. Addresses on that road only go to the 900s."

"What does that mean?" Jennifer asked.

"It means this license is a fake," Sam answered.

AFTER ANOTHER HOUR AT THE school listening to Kristen, Riley and the rest of the officers and deputies who'd arrived on scene interviewing the other students and teachers, Sam had a much better idea of what had transpired that morning.

Kristen's theory had proved right; at least three of the other students and one of the assistant teachers had noticed the guard leading Kristen away from the playground. Nobody had thought anything about it, assuming Maddy had become upset and the guard had decided to take her away from the commotion to calm her down.

"This guy knew just how to pull this off," he murmured to Kristen later at his house. She'd suggested that they go there after they stopped at the police station to drop off the evidence and make extra copies of the security guard's fake license. Kristen figured Grant Mitchell or whoever he really was would probably call Sam there with further instructions.

She sat on the sofa beside him, studying the photo. The Chickasaw County Sheriff's Department had offered their services setting up a tap on the phone in case the kidnapper called, so there wasn't much left for either of them to do but sit and wait to hear from the man who had his daughter.

"I keep thinking I've seen this guy before," she said distractedly. "I don't think I've met him, though. Just—seen him. Like maybe a photo or—" She stopped short, her brow furrowing. "I wonder—" She started to dig in her pockets of her jacket, first the left, then the right.

"What are you looking for?"

She came up empty-handed. "I may have left it in my other jacket at home. It was a photo that Dr. Sowell gave me—he's the doctor who's treating my mother at Darden. Anyway, he gave me a copy of a screen grab from the surveillance cameras at the facility, a picture of the man who visited my mother the other day—the one who took her that newspaper clipping about the attack on Cissy and Maddy."

Sam felt the first niggle of hope he'd had in a couple of hours. "Could it have been the same man?"

"I'm not sure. He didn't have a mustache, and I don't think his hair was as dark as the guy calling himself Grant Mitchell." She gave a little growl of frustration. "Where is that damned photo?"

"Could it be in your car?" Sam suggested.

"I'll go look." She jumped up from the sofa and ran out the door.

Sam picked up the photocopy and stared at the phony driver's license, trying to picture the man with lighter hair and no mustache. A memory danced around the shadowy edges of his mind but wouldn't come out into the light.

His cell phone beeped, the signal for a text message. He pulled his phone from his pocket and punched a couple of buttons. Five words showed up in the display window:

BELLEWOOD MFG 730 2NITE ALONE.

Sam's heart stuttered, then began to race.

Kristen burst through the front door, slightly out of breath but grinning. "Found it." She crossed the room in a coltish bound and dropped onto the sofa beside him.

He quickly tucked his phone into his pocket. *Alone,* the message had said.

No one else could know.

"Any news?" Kristen asked, following his movement with her sharp blue eyes.

He shook his head, trying to look calm even though his insides had turned to ice. "Nothing. Is that the picture?"

She showed him the grainy photo. The photo showed only the side of the man's face, but it was enough. The elusive memory that had been nagging him for the past few minutes crashed into full view, bringing with it both enlightenment and a heavy, crushing sense of despair. He knew the man in the photo. And now he understood the meaning of "Your child for mine."

Ten years ago, at a snowy staging area in Kaziristan, Sam had killed this man's son.

Chapter Sixteen

The look on Sam's face made Kristen's blood freeze. "You know who he is, don't you?"

Sam looked up at her, his expression bleak. "His name is Stan Burkett. I killed his son."

"You killed—how? When?" The ice flooding her veins spread to her skin, raising goose bumps on her arms and legs. Her hand shook as she reached for Sam's hand.

He eluded her touch, rising from the sofa. Apparently he'd found the nervous energy that had just drained out of her; he kept moving as he spoke. "It was ten years ago, in Kaziristan." He stopped pacing long enough to look at her. "There'd been an earthquake, and we'd sent in the Marines to help with the search and rescue, carry emergency supplies—you know the drill."

She nodded. "I remember that."

He went back to pacing. "I was there because I was assigned to the humanitarian mission as a legal liaison. Some of the kids who went over there were fresh out of boot camp at Parris Island. This was their first overseas assignment. Richard Burkett was one of them. Nineteen, with a chip on his shoulder. He got crossways with his CO, a real tough guy— Captain Kent Sullivan." Sam's lips curved slightly. "Sully was hard but fair. Most of the other Marines respected that, but Burkett was convinced Sully was picking on him specifically. Burkett had a temper. And a weapon."

"Burkett fragged Sullivan?" Kristen asked, guessing ahead.

Sam stopped and looked at her. "He tried to. I stopped him with my service weapon." He seemed to have run out of steam, dropping heavily into the armchair across from her. "He was a second away from blowing off Sully's head with an M16 rifle. I didn't have a choice."

"But Burkett's father didn't see it that way?"

"I was cleared by a JAGMAN investigation. I had acted within reason. But Burkett yelled cover-up, claimed the investigation cleared me because I was one of them. He raised a stink but it never went anywhere." Sam ran his hand over his face, his palm rasping against the beard stubble darkening his jaw. "He went away after a few months. I thought that was the end of it."

Kristen crossed to the chair and crouched in front of him, taking his hands in hers. "Not exactly the break in the case you wanted, huh?"

He squeezed her hands, his gaze meeting hers,

dark with fear. "If he's been nursing this grudge this long, he's dangerous. And he has Maddy."

"But it's not really Maddy he wants, right? The note in the backpack said it's you he's after. So he's not going to hurt her while there's a chance to use her to get to you. He's going to be in touch again soon, and then we can figure out how to catch him and get Maddy back."

Sam dropped his gaze to their hands. "Yeah."

She felt the tension in the room rise a few notches, reminding her of the furtive way Sam had tucked his phone in his pocket a few minutes earlier. What wasn't he telling her?

Had he already heard from Burkett?

"Sam, has he already contacted you?"

There was the faintest hesitation before he spoke. "No."

Now she knew he was lying. He'd been holding the phone when she came back in the house, as if he'd just rung off. She'd figured it was one of his family, or maybe Riley Patterson.

What if it had been Burkett?

"Kristen, can you do me a favor?" Sam finally looked up, meeting her gaze. "I need to stick around here, in case a call comes in, but we could really use a little more background information on Burkett. Find out where he's been the last few years, what he's been up to. You have resources at the police department, and I trust you to be thorough. Will you do that for me? And see if Foley's gotten anything out of Darryl Morris."

He might be lying, but the plea she heard in Sam's words was genuine. He was right, too—looking into Stan Burkett's recent activities would be helpful. It might help them figure out where he'd be keeping Maddy, for one thing.

But deep down, she knew that Sam really just wanted her to leave him alone for a while so he could do whatever it was Burkett had told him to do.

She knew confronting him would be useless. If he thought meeting Burkett's demands would save Maddy, he'd do it and lie to God himself about it.

And she'd lie to save them both.

"I'll do that," she answered finally, rising to her feet. She reached out her hand. "Go take a shower or something while I'm gone. It'll help you relax."

"I don't think anything can do that," Sam said bleakly, but he took her hand and let her pull him to his feet.

She tugged at his suit jacket. "Give it a try anyway."

He let her pull his jacket off. She draped it over her arm and turned him toward the hallway. "Go. I'll let myself out."

"Call if you learn anything," Sam said.

"And you call if you hear anything from Burkett."

"I will," Sam lied over his shoulder as he headed toward the bathroom down the hall. Kristen heard a hint of regret in his voice. She supposed she could find a little comfort in knowing he didn't enjoy lying to her.

Suddenly, he turned around and strode back to her, wrapping his hand around the back of her neck. Pulling her to him, he bent his head and kissed her, hard and hungry, his fingers threading through her hair to hold her still while he drank his fill. He drew away, finally, resting his forehead against hers, his breath fast and warm against her cheeks. "I know you wanted off this case, but thanks for staying with it. It means a lot."

For a moment, she thought about nothing but the feel of his body against hers, warm and powerful, yet vulnerable to her touch. It made her feel guilty for what she was about to do—but not guilty enough to change her mind.

He dropped a last, soft kiss on her forehead as he let her go. "I'll see you tomorrow."

"Go take your shower," she whispered.

After he'd disappeared down the hallway, she unfolded his coat, reached into the breast pocket and pulled out his cell phone. The most recent activity had been a text message:

BELLEWOOD MFG 730 2NITE ALONE.

She stared at the message, her heart racing. Bellewood Manufacturing had once been a textile mill on Catawba Road, out past the old dam bridge. No longer in business, the abandoned mill was secluded, well away from prying eyes. By seven-thirty tonight, darkness would have fallen, giving anyone lying in wait at the mill an extra advantage. And Sam believed he'd be going there to meet Burkett alone.

Like hell.

Kristen put the cell phone back in Sam's pocket and draped the coat over the arm of the sofa, wondering what to do next. Wait for him to come out of the shower and confront him with what she knew? Threaten to take him into protective custody to keep him from trying to go out there alone?

One thing she wasn't going to do was let Stan Burkett lay a trap for Sam to walk into.

She let herself out of Sam's house, reaching into her pocket for her cell phone. Carl Madison answered on the first ring. "Madison."

"Carl, it's me." Kristen slid behind the wheel of the Impala. "I need your help."

SAM DIDN'T THINK BURKETT would leave another message before the meeting that evening—the one succinct message he'd sent had been sufficient to set Sam's nerves on permanent alert, which he suspected had been Burkett's intention. But he couldn't take chances, so he checked his cell phone as soon as he got out of his shower.

As he'd expected, nothing from Burkett. But his sister Hannah had left a message. "I'm on my way over." He glanced at his watch. He barely had time to dress before she would arrive.

He let her in after the first couple of bangs on the door and staggered beneath the force of her tackle-hug.

"Tell me what you want me to do," Hannah said without preamble, grabbing his hand and dragging him to the sofa. She was five months pregnant and, thanks to hormones, had two speeds these days, high and supersonic.

"There's nothing to do. The police are all over this, including your cowboy cop. I'm just waiting like everyone else for news."

Hannah's eyes narrowed. "That's a load of bull manure."

"Riley is rubbing off on you."

"No way you're just waiting around for news, Sam Cooper. You're up to something." She scooted closer. "What is it?"

"If I had a supersecret plan, do you think I'd tell you, the biggest blabbermouth in the family?"

"That was twenty years ago," she protested. Her eyes widened suddenly. "You've heard from the kidnapper! What did he do, break in and leave a note under your pillow? I know he didn't call the house or Riley would already know about it. Oh! Your cell phone. He called your cell phone!"

Sam stared at his sister, wondering why she wasn't the cop in the family. "I have no idea what you're talking about."

"You can't go by yourself," she said firmly. "I'll call Riley. He can back you up—"

He caught her hand before she could pull her cell phone from her jacket pocket. "No, Hannah."

She shot him a fierce look. "You're not meeting that bastard alone, Sam. And don't even try to tell me that's not what you have in mind, because you never were any good at lying." Her expression softened. "You're the white knight, Sam. This family needs a white knight. You can't go get yourself killed."

He felt his control beginning to crumble. "He has my baby, Hannah. What else am I supposed to do?"

"Let Riley back you up."

"I can't risk it. Stan Burkett is a former cop—"

Hannah's eyes widened again. "Stan Burkett? The guy whose son—"

"Yes," he interrupted.

"My God." Hannah's expression grew instantly grim. "That explains the note—'your child for mine.'"

Sam nodded. "He'll be looking for signs of police presence. He knows how that works. I can't chance it, not even with Riley. You get that now, don't you?"

He could see that his sister wanted to argue, but she finally nodded. "What time are you meeting him?" she asked.

"I can't tell you that."

She sighed with frustration. "Can you at least tell me if it's today?"

"If you don't hear from me by midnight tonight, you can tell Riley what's going on."

"But we won't know where to look for you."

"I'll leave a message for you. What to do in case you don't hear from me." It wasn't a bad idea, really. If something went wrong, he'd want people to know where to look to get back on Burkett's trail. He could use a free text message scheduling service to leave messages for Kristen and his family. Just to be safe.

Hannah looked as if she still wanted to argue, but she kept her protest to herself, instead pulling him in for a hug. He felt her pregnancy bump against his stomach and smiled in spite of his tension.

"Please be careful," she said.

"I promise, I will. I'm all Maddy has, you know."

But that wasn't true, was it? Maddy had her grandparents, her aunts and uncles. She even had Norah, in a pinch.

And she had Kristen, whether the stubborn detective was ready to admit it or not.

Hannah stayed with Sam a little longer, distracting him with chatter about all the local gossip and goings-on he'd missed during his years away from Gossamer Ridge. Of all his brothers and sisters, Hannah seemed the one most wedded to their hometown, to the beauty of the mountains and the bounty of Gossamer Lake.

When she'd fallen in love with the cowboy cop who'd saved her life when her Wyoming vacation had gone horribly wrong, there had been little discussion about where they'd end up once they said

"I do." Riley had sold his property to his friend Joe Garrison, loaded his two horses in a trailer behind his truck and headed south to Alabama and a new life with his bride.

Sam wished he could tell Riley what he was doing, he reflected later after Hannah had left. Hell, he wished he could tell Kristen. Lying to her about the text message had bothered him a hell of a lot more than keeping it a secret from the rest of the police. She'd put herself on the line for him and Maddy, more than once. She deserved his trust.

She deserved the truth.

But he couldn't tell anyone what he had planned. Not until he had Maddy safely back in his arms.

CARL MADISON GOT INTO the passenger seat of Kristen's Impala and reached for the seat belt. The dashboard clock read seven o'clock on the nose.

"The perimeter's in place." Carl told her. "We're using tracker teams who know the lay of the land. Burkett won't have a clue they're there."

"He'd better not," Kristen answered, her neck already beginning to ache from the unrelenting tension. After passing most of the afternoon working up background information on Stanhope Burkett, she was worried that Sam's decision to go it alone might have been the right one after all.

For one thing, Sam's nemesis was a former St. Louis police officer who probably knew quite a bit about setting traps—and avoiding them. He'd quit the force not long after his son's death and had spent most of the past ten years off the grid, if the lack of a paper trail was anything to go by.

For a while, he'd popped up here and there, speaking to antiwar groups about what he called the "Kaziristan cover-up"—officers getting away with "friendly fire" murders of the enlisted by blaming the victims. But that paper trail had gone cold four years ago after the embassy siege in Kaziristan had changed public sentiment in favor of more military involvement in the area, not less.

The most recent mention of Stan Burkett she'd found was the one that troubled her most, however. The FBI had noted in passing, on a report regarding possible antimilitary activity among some of the more anarchistic antiwar groups, that a man named Stanhope Burkett had been offering survival training to some of the groups for free.

There was no telling where Stan Burkett was keeping Maddy or how easily he might see through Carl's carefully positioned perimeter. She had no idea what he'd do if he spotted the trackers or suspected the police were watching.

And worst of all, Sam Cooper was thirty minutes away from walking right into the middle of the whole mess.

She glanced at the clock again. Five after seven. Time seemed to be creeping.

"You holding up okay?" Carl asked.

She nodded. "Just worried."

"You've grown attached to the kid. And her father."

She didn't answer, her mind full of the reasons she'd given Sam for walking away. With Maddy in danger and Sam putting his life on the line, she wasn't nearly as sure now that she was doing the right thing. What if she was turning her back on her best chance at happiness? At a real family?

"Carl," she said aloud, "what do you know about my mother's condition?"

Carl gave her an odd look. "Her condition?"

She forced the words out. "Her madness. Why did she go crazy? Was it a genetic condition?"

He hesitated a moment. "I thought you knew."

She turned to look at him. "Knew what?"

"It was part of her court proceedings. They assessed her condition to see if she could be treated."

She looked down at the scar on the back of her hand, which glowed faintly in the light from the dashboard. "I've never read the case file. I guess I was afraid to." She forced herself to meet Carl's gaze. "What was wrong with her?"

"She had encephalitis a couple of years after Tammy was born. You must have been around eight. She'd have been in the hospital a week or so—do you remember?"

She nodded. That had been a couple of years after her father had left the family for good.

"The encephalitis apparently caused irreparable damage to the part of your mother's brain that controlled her impulses." Carl's expression was gentle.

"She probably started losing her mind immediately, a little at a time."

Kristen felt her whole body begin to tingle as relief washed over her like floodwaters. Encephalitis, not genetics.

Carl reached across the car seat and touched her cheek. "I thought you knew, kitten. Have you been worrying all this time that you'd turn out like your mama?"

She blinked back tears, her throat constricted with emotion. She just nodded.

"Oh, baby."

The radio crackled. "Team Two, in position." A second later, Team One repeated the call-in.

Carl looked at Kristen. "Game on."

She nodded, still trying to process what he'd told her about her mother's condition. She wasn't going to go mad the way Molly Tandy had. And whether or not she could be a good mother was up to her alone.

It changed everything, she realized. The life she'd thought she could never have was a possibility once more.

But not if something happened to Sam Cooper or his daughter.

BELLEWOOD MANUFACTURING'S Gossamer Ridge mill had been out of business almost ten years, and as abandoned buildings do in a small town where nothing exciting ever happened, the old mill had fallen prey to vandals and thieves. Sam spotted the building's timeworn, graffiti-riddled facade as soon as he rounded a curve in the packed-gravel track that had once been the mill's main drive.

He had parked his Jeep a few yards from the main road, near enough that he could make it back quickly if the need to grab Maddy and flee arose, but not so close or so exposed that his car was an easy mark for sabotage. He was playing by Burkett's rules, for the moment, but he wasn't an idiot.

The sun had set about a half hour earlier, days growing longer as June and the hot Alabama summer approached. A half-moon gazed down in cool blue dispassion, hidden more often than not by silver-edged storm clouds gathering in the western sky, heavy with the threat of rain. When the moon disappeared, the path ahead grew as dark as a cave, the lights of civilization too distant and few to temper the gloom of nightfall.

Sam picked his way carefully through the high-growing grass that had once been the mill's front lawn. Broken liquor bottles and cigarette butts littered the ground beneath his feet, a blighted obstacle course on his path to the mill. He cursed as his foot hit the curve of one bottle, twisting his ankle. He bent to rub the aching joint, taking advantage of the chance to double-check the Glock tucked in the holster tied to his ankle.

He'd come alone, as Burkett said.

But he'd also come armed.

The interior of the mill was even darker than the outside, and smelled of dust and old beer. He pulled a small penlight from his pocket and switched it on. The weak beam illuminated only a few feet ahead of him. He saw the broken hulk of a curved wooden reception desk ahead, tumped onto its side, boards missing and gouges dug out of the wood.

Sam turned off the light and listened a moment. He knew he might be walking into a trap, but he'd had no choice. He just wished that whatever Burkett had planned for him, he'd get on with it. He was tired of waiting.

He decided to try the direct approach. "Burkett? Are you here?"

Silence greeted him, thick and cold.

He turned on the penlight again and started a methodical tour of the mill, going from room to room, trying to keep a map of where he'd already been firm in his mind.

He had reached the main floor of the shop, an enormous area littered with the stripped skeletons of what machinery the mill hadn't been able to sell when it closed up shop. It looked eerily like an industrial abattoir, strewn with metal limbs torn from their mechanical bodies and electrical wires disemboweled from their metal husks.

A low hum against his hip made him jerk. He'd left his phone on vibrate in case Burkett had sent him any last-minute text messages, though he'd put all regular calls on automatic forward to his voice mail.

He pulled the phone from his pocket and flipped it open. The display panel lit up. One text message.

His heart in his throat, he accessed the message.

COPS IN WOODS. YOU DIDNT LISTEN.

Sam stared at the words, his body going cold and shaky. Cops in the woods? Had Hannah broken her promise?

He weaved through the mill's maze of hallways and rooms, emerging a few minutes later through the front door and out into the cool evening air. The moon was peeking through the clouds at the moment, shedding pale silver light over the mill and the surrounding woods.

Sam turned a slow circle, looking for movement in the woods. The woods were usually alive at night, birds and small animals rustling leaves and disturbing the underbrush. But the woods around him seemed unnaturally still, as if the animals were lying low and watchful.

Aware of human intruders in their habitat, Sam thought, anger pouring into his body, driving out his earlier fear.

Stealth was pointless now. Burkett was long gone.

"You scared him off!" he shouted as strongly as he could, wanting to be sure whoever was lurking in the woods heard him loud and clear. "Did you hear me? He spotted you. He's not coming. I want to talk to whoever sent you out here. Now!"

There was a long, silent pause, though Sam thought he might have heard a faint burst of static from a radio somewhere in the deep woods. He remained where he was, his heart hammering in his chest, driven by equal parts anger and fear, while his mind raced frantically for some idea what he should do next.

He prayed for another buzz from his cell phone with another chance to meet Burkett's demand, but the phone remained stubbornly still. The number Burkett had texted from was blocked from receiving messages. Sam supposed, in time, the police might be able to trace his messages back to their source,

But he didn't think Maddy had that much time.

Headlights sliced through the gloom, headed slowly up the access road. He heard the hum of the engine, the hiss-pop of tires on the gravel surface, and then the car came into full view. It was a Chevrolet Impala, and Sam knew before the car door opened who he'd see.

But it still hurt like hell when Kristen stepped out and into the headlight beams.

"You read the text message on my phone," he said as she closed the distance between them. He was surprised by how betrayed he felt. "You surrounded this place with cops when Burkett said for me to come alone. Do you have any idea what you've done?"

"Yes," she said. He heard tears in her voice.

"He could kill Maddy."

Kristen froze a few steps away from him. When she spoke, her voice was broken and raw. "I know."

He didn't know what to say to her now. He didn't even know what he felt anymore.

He just knew he couldn't stay here one minute longer.

With one last look back at the abandoned mill, he started walking down the road to his car.

Chapter Seventeen

Kristen pounded Sam's front door, sick with regret and fear. "Let me in, Sam!"

She could feel him on the other side of the door, his anger and his despair, and the knowledge that she was the one who'd done this to him was almost more than she could bear. She'd felt so hopeful just a little while ago, knowing that her fate was in her own hands. But now, every doubt she'd had about taking this case crashed down around her, mingling with her own terror about what might be happening to Maddy right now.

Blood everywhere. Four little bodies, strewn about the house, lying where Mama had left them...

She choked back a sob and slid to the porch, what little energy she had left draining from her in a flood of despair.

She'd done this. Whatever happened to Maddy now, she owned it. She didn't know how she could live with this one. The pain in her chest felt as if her heart were being shredded apart, strip by strip. She could never piece it back together again.

Behind her, the door opened. The wooden porch floor creaked as Sam walked onto the porch and stood beside her.

She couldn't look up at him. She should never have come here in the first place. Apologies were pointless. What she'd done tonight could never be forgiven.

Sam crouched down beside her. "You shouldn't have gone behind my back. I knew what I was doing. If you figured out I was keeping something from you, you should have trusted that I had a good reason."

She forced the words from her aching throat. "I didn't want you to walk into a trap alone."

"I know you were trying to protect me." She felt his hand on her head, his fingers tangling lightly in her hair. "But she's my daughter. I had the right to take that risk for her."

She looked up at him, her heart full of feeling she couldn't contain. "I love Maddy, too, Sam."

A bubble of joy, out of place in the middle of so much fear and dread, caught her by surprise. A watery laugh erupted from her throat as the full weight of emotion crashed over her.

Sam's gaze locked with hers, and she saw that he understood her jumble of emotions, maybe more than she understood them herself. He caught her hands in his. Rising, he pulled her to her feet and wrapped his arm around her shoulder, leading her into the house and over to the sofa. He made her sit, pulling a crocheted throw from the back of the sofa and wrapping it around her. Only then did she realize she was shivering.

"I'm angry with you," Sam told her, his expression tight.

"You should be." Her teeth were chattering a little.

"You're not supposed to agree. You're supposed to argue back." Sam raked his hand through his hair, his movement rapid and agitated. His voice rose. "You're supposed to tell me I was a stupid fool to go out there by myself and you're the cop and you know better. And then I'm supposed to yell at you that you don't know what you're talking about."

She stood up on wobbly knees to face him, understanding. He needed to feel something besides bone-freezing terror. It was the least she could do for him. "He could have been waiting to kill you the minute you walked in that mill, Sam."

"With me dead, he'd have no reason to keep holding Maddy." Sam's gaze lowered, his voice dropping to a hush, as if confessing something he hadn't even admitted to himself before now. "Burkett would have no reason to hurt her, because doing so would no longer hurt me."

"If he'd killed you, I'd have hunted him down for the rest of my life," she answered in a tone just as hushed. "I wouldn't rest until I found him."

Sam's eyes lifted to meet hers. She could see that he understood what she was really admitting. His throat bobbed and he took a hesitant step toward her, his hand outstretched.

But he stopped, an odd look coming over his face. He reached into his pocket, his face a chaos of emotions, and pulled out his cell phone. Kristen could hear the faint buzz of the vibrating phone now, and her heart froze in place.

Sam's shaking fingers punched a couple of buttons. Kristen watched his face grow slack for a second. Then his gaze flew up to meet hers, and she saw the light of hope blazing from his dark blue eyes.

"He wants to meet again."

Kristen didn't ask where or when. She wasn't going to ruin things for Sam a second time. "I should leave, then."

She started toward the door, but he caught her hand, tugging her back around to face him.

"No," he said firmly. "I'm not playing his game his way this time."

She frowned, not understanding. "What do you mean?"

He touched her face with the lightest brush of his fingertips. "This time, Detective, you're gonna have my back."

"I'M NOT SURE HOW HE'S finding all the abandoned buildings in Chickasaw County," Sam said later as he and Kristen went over the plans. It was almost ten o'clock, a half hour before the next rendezvous with Burkett. Old Saddlecreek Church hadn't seen a congregation through its doors for six or seven years, according to Kristen, who knew more about the town's recent history than he did. The congregation had merged with another church closer to town, and attempts to sell the building hadn't met with much success.

Kristen had called the pastor of the new church and gotten the phone number of the former pastor at Saddlecreek, figuring that if anyone knew the layout of the building, he'd be the one. She'd gleaned enough information that they now had a rough but workable floor plan for the main sanctuary, where Burkett's message had directed Sam to come.

"I'll have the text message set up to send," Sam said, programming the message into the phone so that all he'd have to do was punch one button and the message would go to Kristen's phone. "When you get the message, it will mean I have a visual on Burkett and can distract him while you head into the sanctuary through the back."

"I'm going to make my approach on the organ side," Kristen said, pointing to the organ pit on the right side of the floor plan sketch. "Brother Handley said they were able to sell the piano, but the organ was in such disrepair they haven't been able to unload it. It'll give me some cover. Just make sure he's facing the front of the church."

Sam nodded as he put the cell phone back into his pocket. "Ready to go?"

She looked terrified, but also determined, and if

Sam had had any doubts about including her in this plan, that one look would have driven them away. Whatever happened, he knew he'd made the right choice in trusting Kristen.

With his daughter and with his own life.

When this was all over, and Maddy was back with them, safe and sound, his next big project was going to be convincing Kristen they could trust each other with their hearts, as well. And not just for Maddy's sake.

He couldn't bear the thought of telling Kristen Tandy goodbye.

She was silent on the drive through town, her profile like cool white marble tinged with blue from the dashboard lights. He felt her nervous tension all the way across the cab of the Jeep, but he didn't know how to ease her fears when he was a bundle of nerves himself.

Just do your part, Cooper. You know Kristen will move heaven and earth to do hers.

He reached across and touched her hand where it lay on the seat beside her. She gave a little jerk, then relaxed, turning her hand over to twine with his.

"I don't know whether to hope he has Maddy with him or not," she admitted.

He gave her hand a squeeze. "I know. I've decided it'll be easier if she's not there. Then he can't use her as a pawn."

"But what if he won't tell us where she is?"

He released her hand, needing both hands to steer into a sharp curve. "We'll get it out of him."

The approach to Saddlecreek Church was a narrow, winding blacktop road. Sam supposed Burkett had chosen the meeting place for just such a reason—easy to see cars—and people—approaching. As he made the turn onto the access road, Kristen unbelted herself and slid down in the floorboard of the Jeep, out of sight. She would stay there until she received the text message signal.

Sam parked about fifty yards from the front of the church and cut the engine. "Showtime."

"Be careful."

Sam patted his ankle holster. "I will."

He leaned over the seat toward her, until his face was inches from hers. "Be careful, too." He kissed her cold lips, felt them tremble beneath his. Backing away, he met her anxious gaze. "See you soon."

He exited the Jeep and walked the track to the front of the church. A large chain dangled, snapped in two, from the doors of the church. Under closer examination, the cut in the chains looked fresh. And what he'd thought was the reflection of faint moonlight on the dusty blue stained glass windows was actually a light flickering within the building.

Was Burkett inside already?

Sam pulled the door open. It gave a loud creak and a rattle of the chains, so stealth was out of the question. Not that it mattered. Burkett wouldn't have chosen the old church if he'd thought there was a chance Sam could sneak up on him.

The interior of the old sanctuary was dusty and

smelled of rotting wood and fabric. A mouse scuttled across Sam's path, giving him a start, but he kept his cool, scanning the open room to get a quick lay of the land.

Rows of pews lined the sanctuary, a few missing here and there, either scavenged by thieves or sold by the church. The hymnal racks were empty, and on some of the remaining pews, mice, rats or other vermin, including perhaps the human variety, had torn some of the blue velvet seat pads to shreds.

At the front of the sanctuary, the altar table remained, covered by a tattered purple altar cloth with a gold cross stitched in the middle. Atop the altar cloth sat a hurricane lamp with a flickering flame that filled the room with pale gold light and a dozen writhing shadows.

Sam took in all of this in the matter of a couple of seconds, which was all the time he needed to realize a man was sitting on the front pew, just a few feet from the altar.

His heartbeat skyrocketed.

Slowly, the man in the front pew rose. He took his time as he turned around to face Sam.

It was Burkett. And he was holding Maddy tightly in his arms, a knife blade pressed against her throat.

"Daddy?" Maddy croaked. The man squeezed her to him more tightly, and her cry cut off.

"Son of a bitch!" Sam yelled, forgetting about anything but the sight of his daughter in a madman's arms.

"Not one step farther." Burkett's firm voice carried across the distance between them.

Sam froze, his eyes never leaving his daughter's terrified face. "I'm stopped."

"Take your hand out of your pocket."

Sam realized he still had his finger on the cell phone button. And Burkett had his back to the organ pit.

With the slightest flick of his finger, he pushed the message button. Then he slowly drew his hand from his pocket and lifted it into the air, along with his other one.

And prayed Kristen got the message.

CROUCHED IN THE FLOORBOARD of Sam's Jeep, Kristen felt one leg starting to go to sleep, a cool tingle setting in. She shifted her position to return some circulation to the limb, but almost immediately she felt her other leg start to tingle.

How long had Sam been gone? It felt like an hour, though she knew it couldn't have been more than a few minutes.

She lifted her cell phone, checking the time on the display. Only ten-thirty-five. He'd been gone less than ten minutes. But if Stan Burkett was punctual, they might be standing face-to-face this very moment.

"Text me, Sam," she muttered at the stubbornly silent phone. As if in direct response, her cell phone began vibrating, startling her so much that she dropped it between her folded legs and had to contort her body to pick it up again.

She read the message. It was one word.

Go.

Heart pounding, she opened the car door from her crouched position and slipped outside into the cool night air. She allowed herself a stretch, keeping alert for any sign that Burkett might have an accomplice watching from the woods. They'd considered that possibility, and while they'd both agreed he was almost certainly acting alone, she'd had enough training to take care as she circled through the woods to the back of the church building.

There was a small education annex behind the main church building. It was connected to the sanctuary, probably so that churchgoers wouldn't have to cross from their Sunday school classes to the worship service in the cold or the rain. She checked the clip of her Ruger, then made her way into the education annex through a broken window and flicked on the small flashlight she'd stuck in the pocket of her jeans.

The flashlight beam revealed a long, grimy passageway, filled with litter, a few old beer bottles and soft drink cans. *Kids today,* she thought grimly, making her way as silently as she could through the obstacle course of detritus.

She heard the faint sound of voices somewhere ahead. She followed the sound around a corner and found herself in front of a doorless archway. From inside, a faint glow was visible.

Kristen turned off the flashlight. It took a few seconds for her eyes to acclimate to the darkness, but when her vision settled, she entered the archway and found herself in a small anteroom. Across from her stood a set of heavy wooden doors.

The organ-side entranceway to the sanctuary.

To the right of the double doors, another door stood open. It was from this open door that the faint, flickering light came, casting dancing shadows across the anteroom.

Choir loft, she thought. She'd been in the church choir as a kid, an enthusiastic if not particularly talented alto.

She crossed to the open door and looked inside. A set of five carpeted steps led up to an empty choir loft. Standing in this doorway, she more clearly heard the voices coming from the sanctuary.

"You had to know it would end this way sooner or later." That must be Burkett's voice, a low growl full of barely tempered pain. Kristen would have preferred a more dispassionate voice, she realized. The man's old and nurtured anguish made him deadly.

She padded silently up the carpeted steps to the choir loft and paused at the edge of the panel wall that had once hidden the choir from the view of the congregation as they filed into the loft. She dared a quick peek around the edge.

She saw Sam immediately, standing with his hands slightly raised. If he spotted her, he gave no indication. His attention was focused on the front of the altar area, where another man stood with his back to the choir loft.

"I didn't want to kill your son, Mr. Burkett. I did all I could to talk him down. But he was going to pull that trigger."

"Lies!" Burkett's cry was that of an animal in pain. "You hated him for not being a good little soldier and killing on your orders. You slaughtered him for his conscience!"

Just over the top of the man's shoulder, Kristen spotted a head full of dark curls.

Maddy.

She ducked back out of view, leaning against the panel wall. She closed her eyes and breathed silently but deeply.

Now or never, Tandy.

First, a quick change of plans. Going through the double doors and using the organ would ultimately gain her no advantage. Even if the doors didn't creak when she opened them, Burkett would spot her through his peripheral vision before she got anywhere near him. If she wanted to stay behind him until the last minute, she'd have to go through the choir loft.

"I don't care what you do to me, Burkett. If you think I'm guilty, I'll take your punishment. But Maddy didn't do anything to you or your son. Let her go. Let her go right now and I'll do whatever you want."

The desperation in Sam's voice broke Kristen's

heart. She knew he'd say the same thing—and mean it—even if he didn't know she was waiting to make her move.

Daring another quick glance around the edge of the wall, she spotted the small door set into the wooden rail separating the choir loft from the raised preaching dais. It was half-open already, she saw with a quick spurt of excitement. That would make slipping through it soundlessly that much easier.

"She's the only thing you care about, isn't she?" Burkett said just as Kristen made her swift, silent move out from the shelter of the wall panel and onto the main floor of the choir loft. She lifted the Ruger at the ready, treading lightly as the carpeting ended at the edge of the choir loft. She would have to cross a short span of worn vinyl tiles to get to the low door from the loft to the carpeted dais.

"I'll confess what I did," Sam said quickly, his voice rising. He took a couple of steps toward Burkett, giving Kristen her opportunity to make it through the door and onto the dais without Burkett noticing.

Sam didn't even lift his gaze to look at her, his attention laser-focused on Burkett and his small hostage. "I'll tell the truth about what I did. About what we all did. Just let my daughter go. No more innocents need to die."

"I didn't mean to hurt the girl, you know." Burkett took a step toward Sam.

Kristen froze, holding her breath.

"I just wanted to tie her up so that she wouldn't stop me from taking your daughter."

"She's going to be okay. She can tell the authorities that you didn't mean to hurt her."

Kristen eased to the edge of the dais, by the pulpit. In front of the altar table, with its purple velvet cloth and the flickering hurricane lamp was where she wanted to be. It would put her in the perfect position to jump Burkett at the first chance.

"I want my Daddy!" It was the first time Maddy had spoken since Kristen arrived. She sounded hoarse, as if she'd been crying a lot. Kristen felt a surge of pure rage at Burkett for putting Maddy through this nightmare, and she barely restrained the urge to launch herself at Burkett this very second.

"I'm right here, baby," Sam answered his daughter, taking a couple of steps toward her.

"Stop, Cooper."

"You stop, Burkett. Stop tormenting my child."

"Now you know how it feels."

Maddy started wriggling in Burkett's arms, forcing him to tighten his grasp on her. Maddy cried out in pain.

That was it for Kristen. For Sam, as well, for just as she leaped from the dais, she saw Sam flying up the aisle toward Burkett at a dead run.

Kristen's leg hit the hurricane lamp as she jumped, knocking it onto its side. The flame guttered out, plunging the sanctuary into utter blackness just as Kristen landed on her feet only inches behind Burkett.

She heard Maddy screaming, the sound of grunts and blows landed. She groped in the dark until she felt her fingers tangle in short, coarse hair. Burkett's hair, not Sam's. Sam's hair was softer and a little longer.

Grabbing a handful of hair in her fist, she pressed the butt of the Ruger against the back of his head.

"Give Sam his daughter," she said in a low, deadly tone.

She felt movement, and Sam called out, "I've got her."

Kristen let go of Burkett's hair long enough to reach in her pocket for the penlight. But the second Burkett felt her hand move, he whirled around, catching her off guard. He slammed her into the altar with a bone-jarring thud. One of his hands circled her wrist, forcing her gun hand back against the wooden table with a sharp crack.

She tried to keep her grip on the Ruger but her fingers went briefly numb, and the weapon slid from her grasp. She heard it bounce across the altar table and hit the carpeted floor with a muted thud.

"Kristen!" Sam called out.

"Get Maddy out of here!"

She felt a sudden, sharp pain in her side and realized Burkett still had the knife. As he hauled back for another stab, she shifted right and brought her knee up into his groin.

Burkett reeled away, and she scrambled away from his grasp, her side burning as if it was on fire. Her foot connected with something on the floor. The Ruger. She dropped to her knees and found the pistol. Rising quickly, she pulled the penlight from her pocket and switched it on, illuminating the front of the sanctuary.

Burkett staggered toward her, knife in hand. Sam was right behind him, ready to pounce.

"Gun beats knife," Kristen barked, raising the Ruger steadily in front of her, though it took every ounce of waning strength she had. She felt blood spilling from the wound in her side, a hot, wet stream moving over her hip and down her leg.

Sam grabbed the knife from Burkett and threw it into the pews. "Stay back there, Maddy!" he called over his shoulder as he subdued Burkett with the set of plastic flex cuffs Kristen had given him before they left the house.

"You're hurt," he said to Kristen, his eyes wide with fear as he took in the blood pouring from her side.

"I'm okay," she said, but her voice barely registered. Her knees gave out, and she sank to the floor.

The penlight must have broken, she thought as the world went dark again. She thought she heard Sam's voice again, but it was faint and faraway.

Had he left her? Had he taken Maddy and gone far, far away? She struggled to sit up, to find her feet again. She had to go after then. She couldn't let them leave her. She needed them both so much.

Then even sound abandoned her, and she sank into a deep, silent darkness.

WHEN SOUND AND SIGHT RETURNED, they arrived in a cacophony of raised voices and frantic motion. It took Kristen a second to realize she was in a hospital emergency room bay, surrounded by green-clad doctors, nurses and technicians poking, prodding and dragging her out of the peaceful darkness.

"There she is," one of the doctors said, smiling at her. "BP's coming back. She's stabilizing nicely." He bent closer to her. "You're in the Chickasaw County Medical Center, Detective Tandy. Can you talk?"

Kristen's voice came out in a croak. "Where's Sam?"

"Mr. Cooper's just outside. Let us get you all hooked up and settled down here and we'll bring him right in."

Looking down, she saw that she was naked, her clothes lying in strips on a nearby equipment table. Her left side was a screaming ball of agony, but the doctor assured her they had stopped the bleeding and once the blood transfusion was finished, she'd be feeling better in no time.

They covered her with a sheet, finally, and brought Sam into the emergency bay. He was bone-white and looked as though he'd just walked through the pit of hell, but when he locked gazes with her, his face spread into a smile as bright as a clear June morning. He caught her hand in his, lifting her knuckles to his lips for a quick kiss. "You sure know how to make an impression on a guy, Tandy."

"Where's Maddy?" she asked. "Is she okay?"

"She's fine. The doctors just finished checking her out and now she's with my folks in the waiting room. I'll bring her to see you once you're in a room."

"Is someone watching her?" she asked, anxious.

"Riley's playing bodyguard, but it's over now. Burkett's in lockup." Sam stroked her hair, his smile widening. "Half the Gossamer Ridge police force is guarding him. The other half is out in the waiting room, driving the nurses crazy. You have quite an admiration society going on there."

She shook her head. "I blew it back there. I heard Maddy cry out and I lost my head."

"So did I." He stroked a stray lock of hair away from her damp face. "It's what parents do."

Tears pricked her eyes. "I had to protect her, whatever the cost."

"I know."

"I would have done that for my brothers and sisters, Sam. If I'd had an idea what my mother was going to do—"

Sam touched her lips with his fingertips. "I know that, too. You were always too hard on yourself about that."

She pressed her lips to his fingers in a light kiss. "You sound like Carl."

"Carl's a smart man," Sam replied with a smile. "He was smart enough to love you."

She heard the vow hidden in his words. She saw the emotion shining in his eyes. It was crazy, really, to feel so much after such a short time, but she knew it was true.

She felt it herself.

"When you get out of here, we need to talk," Sam said.

She managed a weak smile. "If by 'talk' you mean you're going to tell me how things will be between us from now on, I should warn you I already have a few ideas about that."

He ran his thumb over the curve of her chin. "Really."

"Yeah. Like daily foot rubs. And who gets to drive."

"Daily foot rubs, huh? For you or for me?"

"I suppose it could be a mutual thing," she answered, feeling a little silly being flirtatious while she was lying naked and wounded under a little bitty sheet on a gurney.

"Deal," he said, bending to give her a passionate kiss that made her woozy head reel until the doctor came into the room to shoo him out.

Kristen watched him leave, her heart so full of joy she could hardly breathe. Maddy was safe. Burkett was in custody. And she was crazy in love with a wonderful man just crazy enough to love her back. Had she actually died back there in the abandoned church and gone straight to heaven?

If so, there was nowhere else she'd rather be.

Epilogue

Six months later

They had decided against a big, fancy wedding, opting instead for a smaller lakeside ceremony, with just family and close friends in attendance. The whole Cooper clan was there, except for Sam's brother Luke, who seemed to be the prodigal son. On Kristen's side, there were Carl and Helen, of course, and Jason Foley was there with his very pregnant wife.

"She's promised she won't go into labor during the ceremony," Foley assured Kristen when he found a minute alone with her shortly before the ceremony. "I told her if her water breaks, move closer to the lake and she'll be fine."

"God, you're gross," Kristen said with a grimace, but she gave him a hug anyway. "Thanks for coming."

"Wouldn't miss it, Tandy. I can still call you Tandy, right?"

"For the next twenty minutes." Sam's voice was

close to Kristen's ear. She pulled back from Foley's embrace and beamed up at her husband-to-be.

"Don't you know it's bad luck to see the bride before the wedding?" she teased.

He smiled back. "Looking at you could never be bad luck."

"Ugh. Newlyweds," Foley muttered. He winked at Kristen. "Enjoy this phase while it lasts. Dirty dishes and laundry are just around the bend." He shook Sam's hand, his expression growing serious. "Be good to her."

"I will," Sam promised. He turned back to Kristen after Foley left. She saw that he was holding a box in his left hand. He gave it to her. "I brought you a prewedding gift."

She examined it. It was a sturdy cardboard box, unwrapped. About the size of a tissue box. Whatever lay inside was heavy.

"Don't shake it and don't drop it," Sam warned. "Need my help opening it?"

"I can do it," she said, even though her hands were shaking a little. Prewedding jitters, she supposed, although after six months of courtship by both Sam and Maddy, she was finally sure this marriage was the right thing for all of them.

The box opened easily from the top. Inside, she found a clear jar filled with water and a small cutting from a rosebush. Her bittersweet childhood memory came rushing back, more sweet than bitter for the first time.

She looked up at him through a film of tears. "I can't believe you remembered that story."

He grinned at her, clearly pleased with himself. "Your neighbor still lives in the same house, you know. She still has the same rosebushes."

She stared at him. "You got this from Mrs. Tamberlain?"

"She was happy to hear you were getting married and sends her best wishes." He leaned closer. "Do you like it?"

She felt tears spill down her cheeks, probably ruining her makeup, but she didn't care. "It's perfect."

"I thought about buying you a brand-new bush," he admitted, pulling out his handkerchief and wiping the tears away, "but I decided I wanted to give you something that showed you how much faith I have in you. In us."

She didn't need proof of that, of course. He'd shown his faith in her when he'd asked her to be part of his and Maddy's lives. But she understood what he was telling her with this beautiful, unique gift.

He was entrusting her with something delicate and fragile, just like the rose cutting. Something that would need nurturing, attention and care.

He was entrusting her with Maddy. And with his own heart.

"I love you," she whispered, rising on tiptoe to brush her lips against his.

He tugged her close, his arms wrapping tightly

around her waist. "Love you back," he murmured against her ear.

Behind his back, she lifted the jar of water holding the rose cutting to look at it again. Sunlight slanted through the windows of the room, making the water sparkle like diamonds.

And at the bottom of the cutting, she saw with delight, the first little root had begun to sprout.

* * * * *

Rancher Ramsey Westmoreland's temporary cook is way too attractive for his liking.
Little does he know Chloe Burton came to his ranch with another agenda entirely....

That man across the street had to be, without a doubt, the most handsome man she'd ever seen.

Chloe Burton's pulse beat rhythmically as he stopped to talk to another man in front of a feed store. He was tall, dark and every inch of sexy—from his Stetson to the well-worn leather boots on his feet. And from the way his jeans and Western shirt fit his broad muscular shoulders, it was quite obvious he had everything it took to separate the men from the boys. The combination was enough to corrupt any woman's mind and had her weakening even from a distance. Her body felt flushed. It was hot. Unsettled.

Over the past year the only male who had gotten her time and attention had been the e-mail. That was simply pathetic, especially since now she was practically drooling simply at the sight of a man. Even his stance—both hands in his jeans pockets, legs braced apart, was a pose she would carry to her dreams.

And he was smiling, evidently enjoying the conversation being exchanged. He had dimples, incredibly sexy dimples in not one but both cheeks.

"What are you staring at, Clo?"

Chloe nearly jumped. She'd forgotten she had a lunch date. She glanced over the table at her best friend from college, Lucia Conyers.

"Take a look at that man across the street in the blue shirt, Lucia. Will he not be perfect for Denver's first issue of *Simply Irresistible* or what?" Chloe asked with so much excitement she almost couldn't stand it.

She was the owner of *Simply Irresistible*, a magazine for today's up-and-coming woman. Their once-a-year Irresistible Man cover, which highlighted a man the magazine felt deserved the honor, had increased sales enough for Chloe to open a Denver office.

When Lucia didn't say anything but kept staring, Chloe's smile widened. "Well?"

Lucia glanced across the booth at her. "Since you asked, I'll tell you what I see. One of the Westmorelands—Ramsey Westmoreland. And yes, he'd be perfect for the cover, but he won't do it."

Chloe raised a brow. "He'd get paid for his services, of course."

Lucia laughed and shook her head. "Getting paid won't be the issue, Clo—Ramsey is one of the wealthiest sheep ranchers in this part of Colorado. But everyone knows what a private person he is. Trust me—he won't do it."

Chloe couldn't help but smile. The man was the epitome of what she was looking for in a magazine cover and she was determined that whatever it took, he would be it.

"Umm, I don't like that look on your face, Chloe. I've seen it before and know exactly what it means."

She watched as Ramsey Westmoreland entered the store with a swagger that made her almost breathless. She *would* be seeing him again.

* * * * *

Look for Silhouette Desire's
HOT WESTMORELAND NIGHTS
by Brenda Jackson,
available March 9 wherever books are sold.

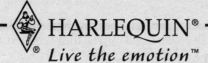

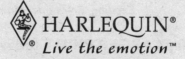

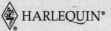

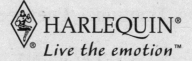

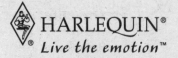